This Book Belongs To

____

First published in 2024 by The Curious Writer

ISBN 978-1-0687364-1-4

CONTENTS

TCW

Elevating Creativity and Knowledge

"Curiosity is the essence of human existence"
- Gene Cernan (NASA Astronaut)

Unless credited, all other visuals have been created using cinematic visual effects (VFX) techniques by the Author and authorised images. Purposes of the visuals are to capture the essence of celestial objects and provide a splendour of stimulating imagery that unlocks the imagination and educates the next generation of explorers and thinkers.

Are you ready?

Let's go!

Welcome Aboard!

Welcome aboard! My name is Leonardo, but my friends call me Leo!

I'm an astronaut, and I will be your pilot on this adventure. I'm going to be at the back of the spaceship flying! But I'll be here to keep you safe and make sure you have the best journey! Lucky you - you're going to be at the front for the best views!

You can use your reference card to help you along the way, as we first pass through our solar system and then onto intergalactic space.

Anyway, without further ado, are you ready?

Let's go!

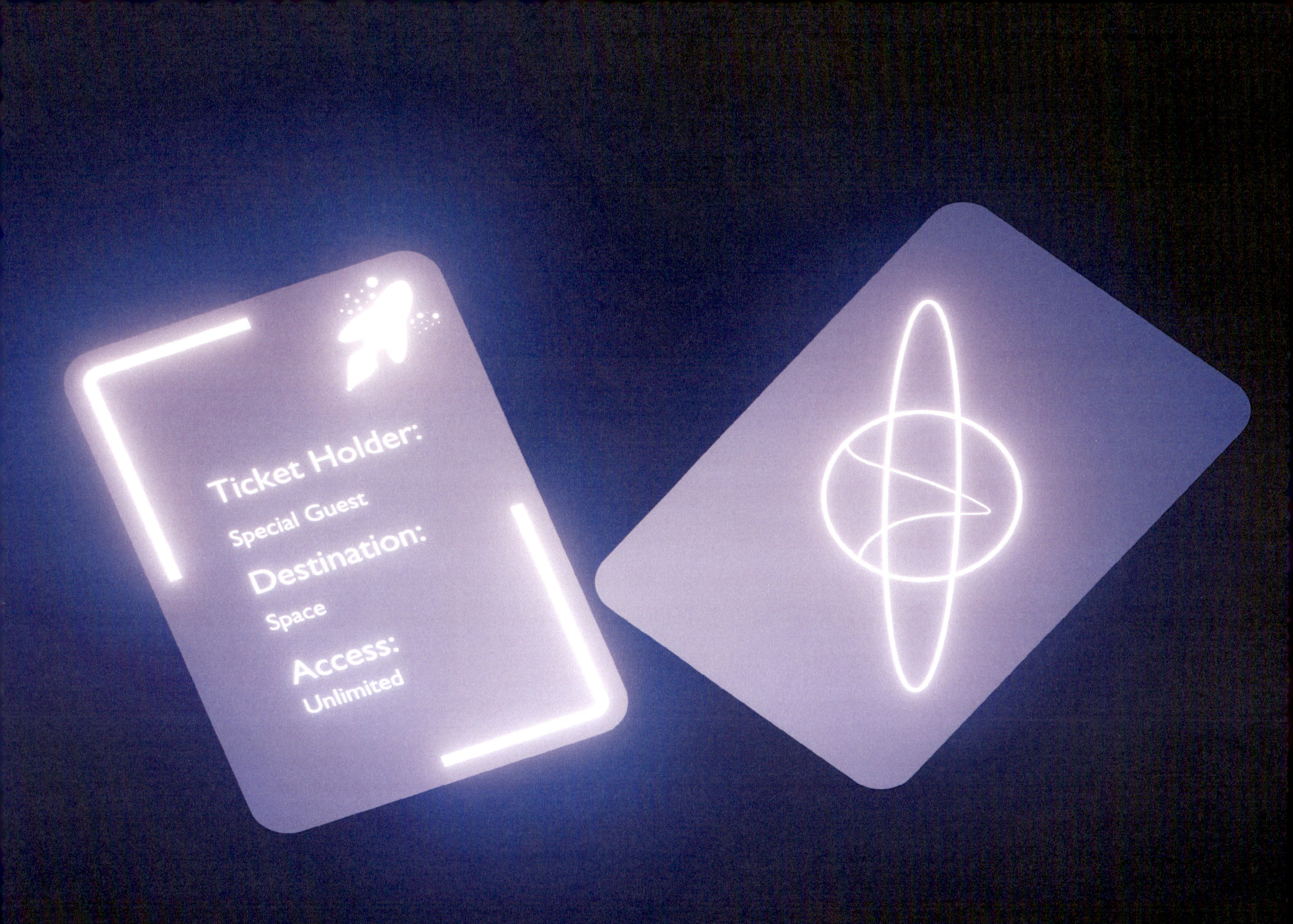
Ticket Holder:
Special Guest
Destination:
Space
Access:
Unlimited

Reference Card

* Light year = distance travelled by light in 1 year = 9.4 trillion kilometres !

* Particle = tiny bits of matter.

* Atom = basic particles that make chemicals.

* Subatomic particles = tiny particles that are smaller than an atom, and make up all matter.

* Scientist = a person who studies one or more of the natural sciences (physics, chemistry, or biology).

* Engineer = derived from the old Latin and English words to mean 'contrive' and 'cleverness', an engineer is a person who solves real-world problems and invents, designs, builds, analyses, and tests technology to help change the world.

Scientific Notation	Number	Name
10^0	1	One
10^1	10	Ten
10^2	100	One Hundred
10^3	1,000	One Thousand
10^6	1,000,000	One Million
10^{10}	10,000,000,000	Ten Billion
10^{24}	1,000,000,000, 000,000,000, 000,000	Septillion

1 kilometre (km) = 1000 metres (m) = 0.62 miles (mi)

1 kilometre per hour (km/hr) = 0.62 miles per hour (mph)

1 kilometre per second (km/s) = 2236.94 miles per hour

1 kilogram (kg) = 2.20462 pounds (lbs)

FIRST STOP: OUR SOLAR SYSTEM

Earth!

Home Sweet Home!

A place like no other, Earth is the third planet from the Sun, and it is where we call Home!

The temperature is just right for liquid water to form and support life! Water is extremely precious for us, and it is made up of hydrogen and oxygen atoms. Did you know that around 71 percent (%) of the Earth's surface is covered with water! That is a lot!

Notice that thin blue line near the top of the earth? That's our atmosphere! It is what keeps us alive and protects us from the harshness of space! It is mainly made up of nitrogen, oxygen, and argon elements that allow humans, animals, and plants to breathe and stay alive with the help of the Sun!

Did you know that Earth's escape velocity is 11.2 kilometres/second? This is how fast we must travel in a rocket to go into outer space!

EARTH's CHARACTERISTIC	VALUE
Mass (kilograms)	5.972×10^{24}
Approximate diameter (kilometres)	12.7×10^{3}
Escape velocity (kilometres/second)	11.2
Distance from the Sun (kilometres)	149×10^{6}
Planet number from the Sun	3

Look it's the 'Terminator' line! This is the region where day meets night· It is also known as the 'Twilight Zone'·

Earth!

Our atmosphere looks blue because the blue part of the light spectrum from the Sun's light is scattered by the particles in the air. Cool!

There are nearly 24 hours in a day on earth. But when you're having fun with other people time seems to fly by! Speaking of which, we forgot to mention that as of the year 2024 the human population is just over eight billion! Think of how many people that is! That means if you spent one minute talking to every single person alive it would take approximately 15,000 years to finish speaking! WOW!

Did you know that according to the evidence we have, human life started on the continent of Africa?!

Earth is the most beautiful place in the universe - but if you could make the world a better place what would you do?

The International Space Station!

The International Space Station

The International Space Station or ISS was constructed between 1998 and 2011, and it is the most expensive engineering project the world has ever seen, costing roughly 150 billion US dollars!

Designed and constructed between the USA, Canada, Japan, and Europe (including Russia), its purpose was to be a space lab that would allow science experiments to be performed by astronauts in 'micro gravity' and space environments.

It has allowed us to understand so many cool and practical areas of science from drug development using protein crystals, understanding various human diseases and health, to understanding the 5th state of matter (plasma), and gaining a new perspective on Earth and our place in the universe!

Did you know that the ISS is resupplied with food, water, fuel, and other scientific equipment every three months?

Did you know that the first people to live on the ISS were astronaut Bill Shephard and cosmonauts Yuri Gidzenko and Sergei Krikalev?

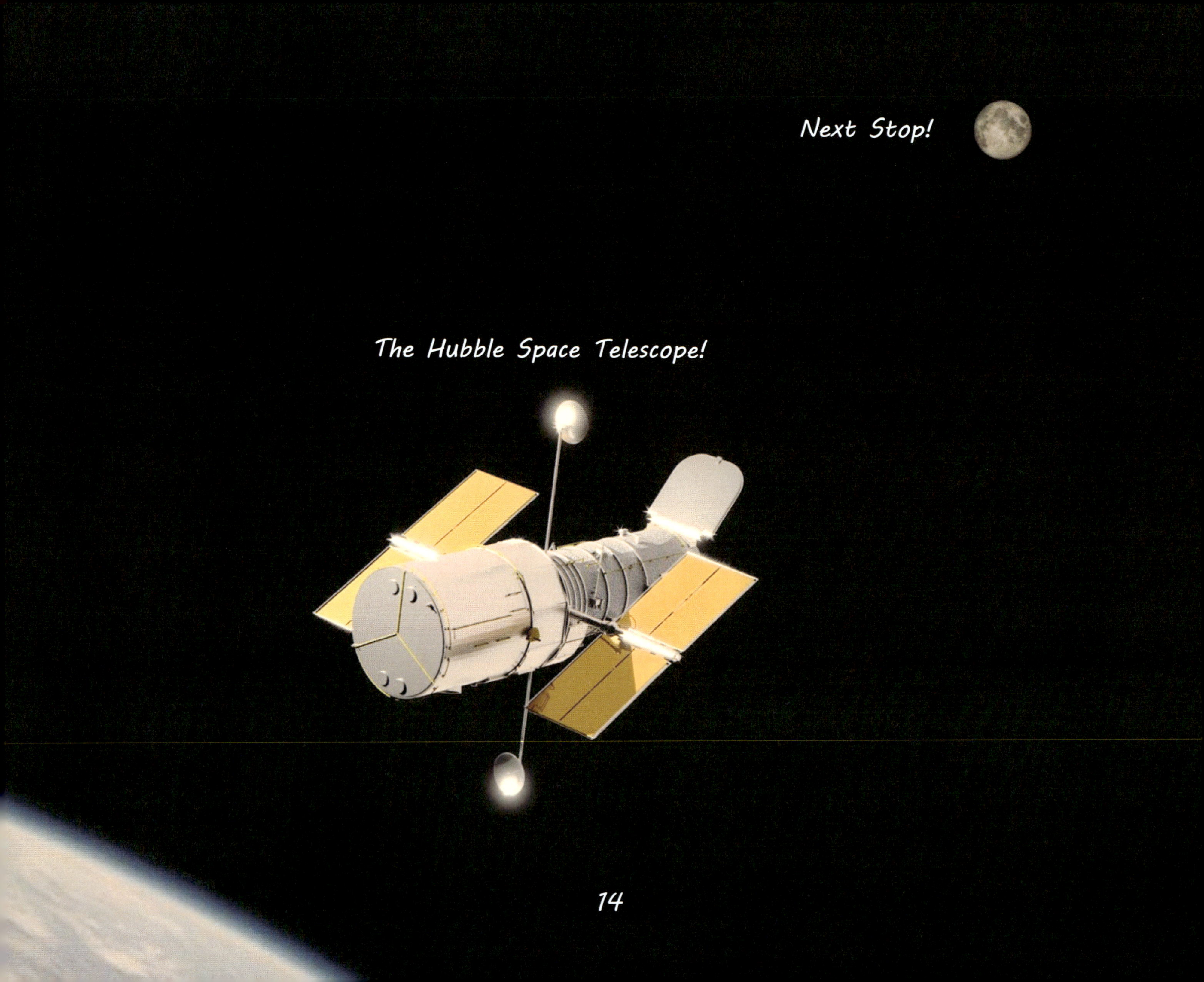
Next Stop!
The Hubble Space Telescope!

The Hubble Space Telescope

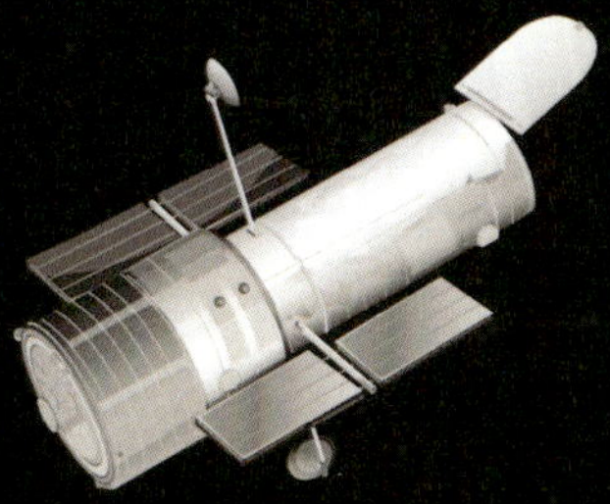

The Hubble Space Telescope (HST), named after the famous scientist Edwin Hubble, is a testament to the ingenuity of scientific instruments and the human space program.

Launched on April 24th, 1990, the HST has absolutely changed humanity's view and understanding of the universe! From discovering new planets to picturing some of the most awe-inspiring regions of space that were never seen before, the HST allowed new types of space-based data to be collected in detail.

The purpose of putting the telescope in Earth orbit was to simply get away from the disturbances and influence of our atmosphere, including light pollution. This way, images are crystal clear! =)

The main reason for building and launching HST was to measure the size and age of our universe!

Did you know that when the first images were taken, scientists found that Hubble was short sighted?!!!

NASA had to fix the issues with the mirror and instruments! They gave it glasses! =)

This deep field image of the galaxy cluster MACSJ0717.5+3745 was taken by the Hubble Space Telescope! It shows thousands of galaxies and light being bent because of gravity! Cool!

The Butterfly Nebula, Located within our galaxy, about 3800 light years away!

This spectacular image was taken after astronauts installed a new camera on Hubble in 2009.

Dust lanes and star clusters in the elliptical galaxy NCG 1316, pictured by Hubble!

Look! It's 'Point Nemo'!

This is the most inaccessible place over water, on Earth!

It lies in the Southern Pacific Ocean, about 50° south and 120° west.

Our Home! Nicknamed 'The Blue Marble'. Doesn't she look Beautiful!

The Moon

A friendly face - the moon is our closest neighbour in our solar system. If you look up at the moon on a clear night, you can see its amazing craters and dark areas called 'Maria', named after the Latin word to mean seas! The moon is not a planet. It is considered a natural 'satellite' that orbits around its host planet, Earth.

As of 2024 only 12 humans have ever walked on the moon!

The first human to walk on the moon was NASA astronaut Neil Armstrong, on July 20th, 1969!

Did you know that it takes about three days to reach the moon in a spacecraft?!

THE MOON'S CHARACTERISTIC	VALUE
Mass (kilograms)	$0{\cdot}0735 \times 10^{24}$
Approximate diameter (kilometres)	$3{\cdot}5 \times 10^{3}$
Escape velocity (kilometres/second)	2·4
Distance from Earth (kilometres)	384×10^{3}
Time to complete one orbit	27·3 days

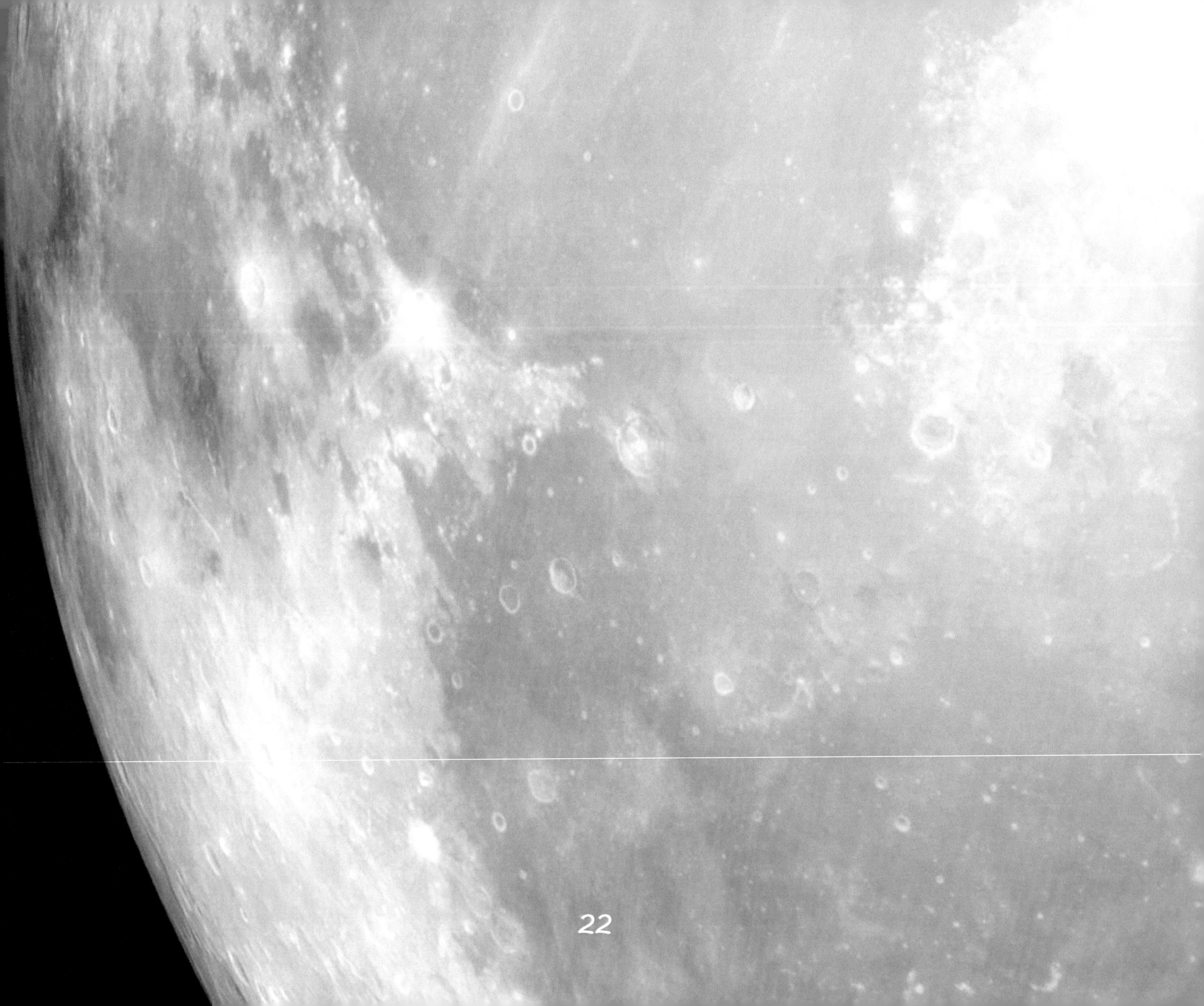

The Moon

Scientists think that in its early formation another planet collided with Earth! The debris and rocks that formed after the collision merged in Earth's orbit and created the moon!

It turns out that our moon is slowly moving away from Earth! This is because of tidal forces, due to gravity, causes the Earth to slow down and the moon to speed up and move slowly away from us. =(

Here's something cool - it is because of the moon that we have tides on our oceans and seas! Tides are the rise and fall in ocean and sea water levels due to gravitational forces.

Humans will soon return to the moon, and perhaps create a lunar base for scientific research and engineering projects. Cool!

What would you do if you had the chance to go to the moon? And what type of lunar-based work do you think will help humans back on Earth?

Mercury

Mercury is the closest planet to the Sun! Unlike Earth, it has no moons and atmosphere of its own· =(

It is also the smallest planet in our solar system and because it is so close to the Sun, it only takes 88 days for one year! That means on Mercury you will see your birthday faster, compared on Earth! =)

Robot spacecrafts named Mariner 10 and Messenger have been to Mercury! They flew around the planet and took images to help us see what it looks like up close· New spacecrafts from the European and Japanese space agencies are soon expected to take more detailed observations of the planet·

Did you know that the element Mercury is commonly used in thermometers to measure temperature?

MERCURY'S CHARACTERISTIC	VALUE
Mass (kilograms)	0·328 x 10^{24}
Approximate diameter (kilometres)	5 x 10^{3}
Escape velocity (kilometres/second)	4·3
Distance from the Sun (kilometres)	58 x 10^{6}
Planet number from the Sun	1

Venus

Known as the “morning star’ or ‘evening star’, this awesome planet is named after the ancient Roman goddess of Love!

It is the hottest planet in our solar system and has a thick atmosphere full of carbon dioxide and clouds made of sulphuric acid! Ouch!

Its size is nearly the same as Earth and known to be our sister planet =)·

Scientists study Venus to help them learn about how Earth was created over 4·5 billion years ago!

Did you know that you can see Venus with your naked eye in the western sky just after sunset, or in the eastern sky just before sunrise?! Check it out for yourself! =)

VENUS'S CHARACTERISTIC	VALUE
Mass (kilograms)	$4{\cdot}87 \times 10^{24}$
Approximate diameter (kilometres)	12×10^{3}
Escape velocity (kilometres/second)	10·4
Distance from the Sun (kilometres)	108×10^{6}
Planet number from the Sun	2

Mars

Mars is known as the 'red planet', because of the colour of its surface. But in reality, it is a little brown and orangey. Mars is slightly smaller than Earth and has mesmerized us since its discovery in 1610, by the famous scientist Galileo Galilei.

Human beings are planning to go there one day! Who knows, it might be you! How amazing would that be?

Scientists and engineers have sent many robots to Mars, to help them discover and learn more about the planet. We now understand a lot about its' climate, weather, and geology, from studying rock samples and other atmospheric data.

Did you know that in 2021 NASA flew an autonomous helicopter called 'Ingenuity' on Mars?! This was the very first time a helicopter had flown outside of Earth!

MARS'S CHARACTERISTIC	VALUE
Mass (kilograms)	$0{\cdot}642 \times 10^{24}$
Approximate diameter (kilometres)	$6{\cdot}8 \times 10^{3}$
Escape velocity (kilometres/second)	5·0
Distance from the Sun (kilometres)	228×10^{6}
Planet number from the Sun	4

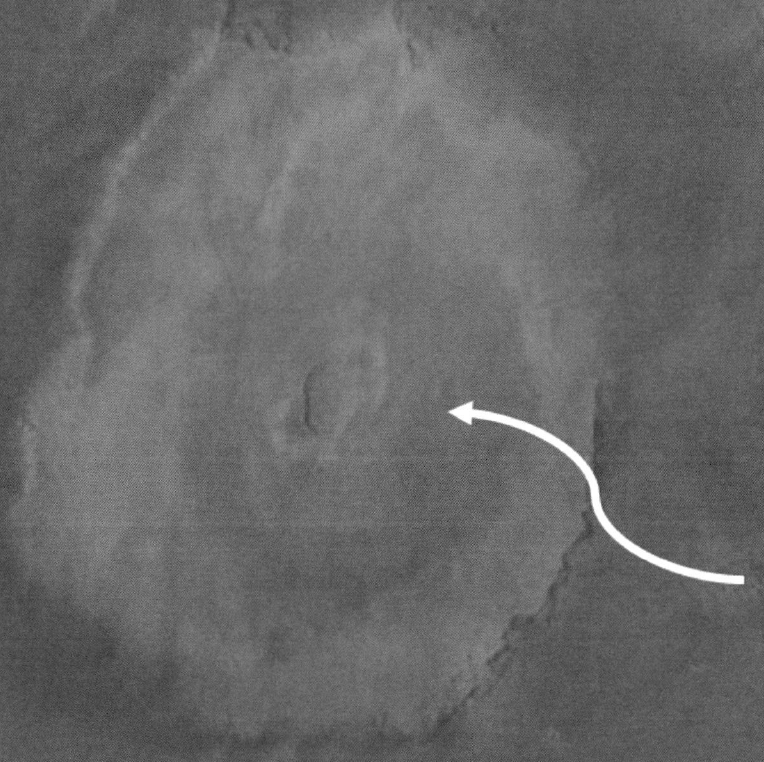

Look, Olympus Mons! It is one of the tallest known mountains in our solar system, with a height of nearly 22 kilometres! That is about 2·5 times taller than mount Everest back on Earth!

Scientists think that there might even be life on Mars! Very tiny bacteria and small organisms· The more we explore, the more we will discover in years to come· Exciting!

What do you think is on Mars? Would you like to explore it one day?

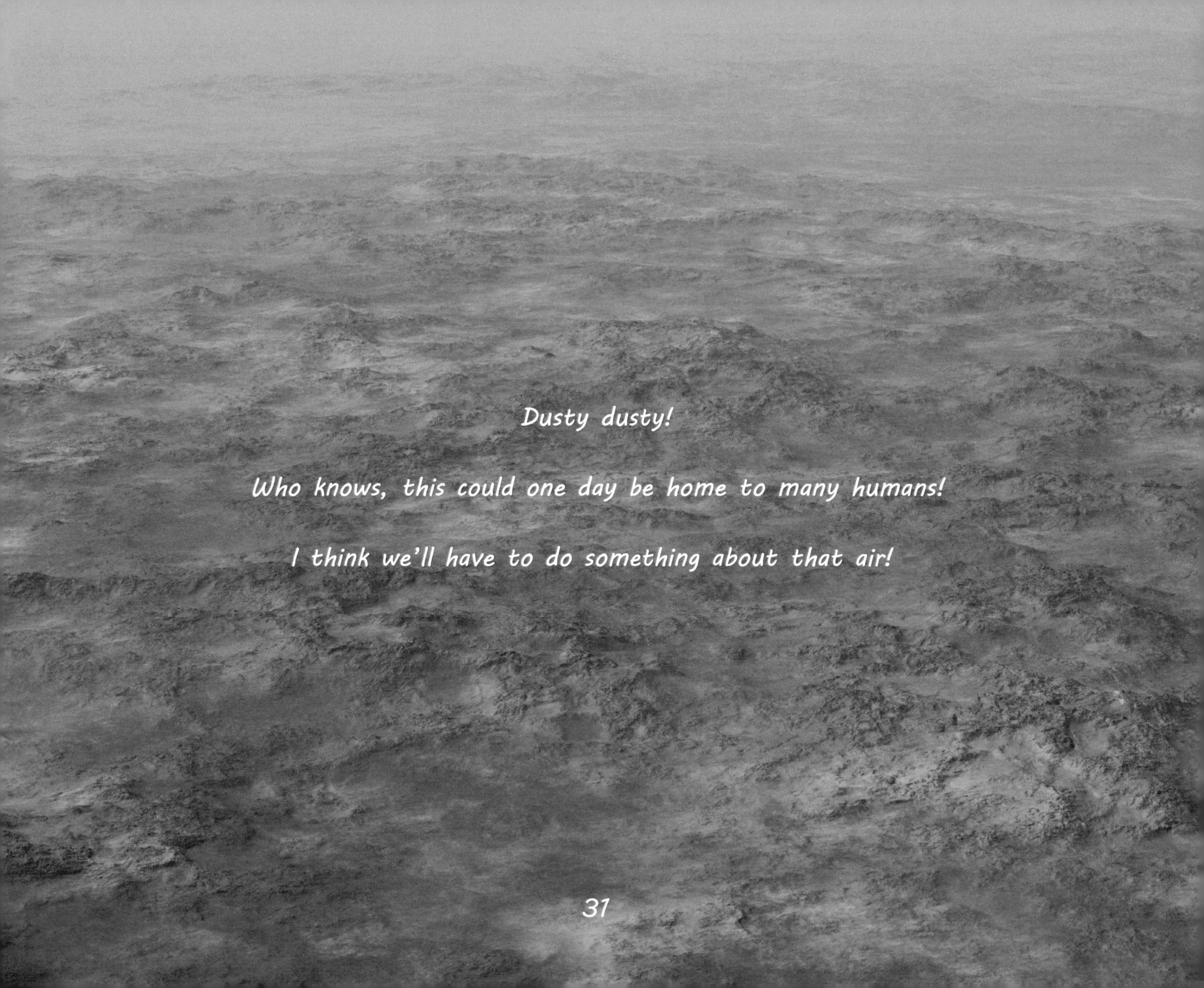

Dusty dusty!

Who knows, this could one day be home to many humans!

I think we'll have to do something about that air!

Hey... It's Leo here! Hold tight!

We are passing through a place called the 'Asteroid Belt'!

Woooo!

Asteroid

The most famous comet, 'Halley's' will next approach Earth in the year 2061!

Asteroids are rocky leftovers from the early formation of our solar system. They vary in size from hundreds of miles across, all the way down to a few meters!

Majority of the asteroids in our solar system sit in the asteroid belt, but a few now and then get thrown off into deep space or towards Earth!

Another name for asteroids is 'minor planet', which is considered any celestial object in orbit around our Sun that is not a planet or comet.

Did you know that in 2001 a NASA spacecraft called NEAR landed on an asteroid named EROS?!

Did you know that there is a difference between asteroids, comets, and meteoroids? Comets are mainly made up of dust and ice, while asteroids are rocky, and meteoroids are small broken bits of asteroids and comets!

Jupiter

A majestic sight - the largest planet in our solar system! Jupiter is so big that it is responsible for saving the other planets from asteroids that come from inside and outside our solar system! He is our big brother! Jupiter is known as a gas giant. It does not have a solid surface like earth, but it may contain a solid centre core.

This planet is so big that you can fit over 1300 earths inside of it!

Jupiter is the name of the ancient Roman god of the sky and thunder, who ruled over the other gods.

Did you know that Jupiter officially has 95 moons?!

JUPITER'S CHARACTERISTIC	VALUE
Mass (kilograms)	1898×10^{24}
Approximate diameter (kilometres)	143×10^{3}
Escape velocity (kilometres/second)	59.5
Distance from the Sun (kilometres)	778.5×10^{6}
Planet number from the Sun	5

The Great Red Spot!

The Great Red Spot

Jupiter's Great Red Spot is an ancient storm that is the largest known in our solar system, and three earths can fit inside of it! It is called an 'anticyclone' because it spins anticlockwise in the planet's southern hemisphere.

Inside the great red spot winds can peak at about 400 miles/hour!!! This storm lies in the upper atmosphere of Jupiter, and it is still unknown how it was created.

Did you know that it is still debated whether the English polymath Robert Hooke, or the Italian scientist Giovanni Cassini really discovered the Great Red Spot first?!

It is still unknown how deep the spot goes. We need more information from our space probes to figure this mystery out!

Saturn

Known as the 'jewel' in our solar system, Saturn boasts its amazing colourful rings that are made up of small and large rocks, icy particles, and other debris that were collected in its early formation.

It is the second largest planet in the solar system, and just like Jupiter it is a gas giant! It has no solid surface and is made up of mainly hydrogen and helium.

Since Saturn's discovery in 1610 by Galileo Galilei, humans have always looked at Saturn and been amazed by its beauty.

Did you know that Saturn is so light that it could float on Earth's oceans?!

SATURN'S CHARACTERISTIC	VALUE
Mass (kilograms)	568×10^{24}
Approximate diameter (kilometres)	121×10^{3}
Escape velocity (kilometres/second)	35·5
Distance from the Sun (kilometres)	1432×10^{6}
Planet number from the Sun	6

Saturn

The name Saturn comes from the ancient Roman god of agriculture and wealth!

rn has 146 known moons! These moons vary in size and humans have sent spacecraft to discover some of them. The most famous moon is called Titan.

ol thing about Titan is that it has an atmosphere, and it is also the only object in space other than Earth where stable surface liquids have been found!

Could some form of alien life be on there? Who knows!

If you discovered Saturn, what would you have called it?

How do you think Saturn's rings were made?

Uranus

Uranus is an ice giant, mainly made up of water, methane, and ammonia fluids. Its atmosphere contains a lot of methane that give this planet it's amazing light blue colour! It even has rings just like Saturn, and 28 moons have been discovered.

It gets extremely cold here. The average temperature is about -195°C (-319°F)!!! That makes it one of the coldest planets in our solar system...Brrrr!

Did you know that scientists believe it could be raining diamonds inside Uranus?! This is due to the immense pressures generated close to the core of the planet.

URANUS'S CHARACTERISTIC	VALUE
Mass (kilograms)	86.8×10^{24}
Approximate diameter (kilometres)	51×10^{3}
Escape velocity (kilometres/second)	21.3
Distance from the Sun (kilometres)	2867×10^{6}
Planet number from the Sun	7

Neptune

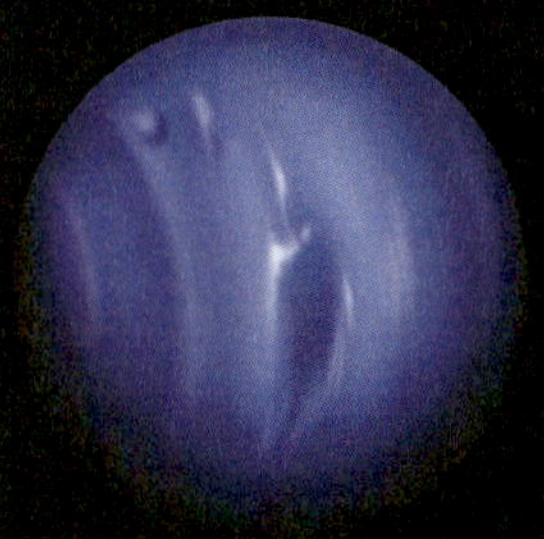

Neptune is the last of the major planets, and the fourth largest in our solar system!

One day on Neptune is only 16 hours! This is because of how fast this planet spins on its axis.

The planet was discovered in the year 1846 by three scientists named Urbain Le Verrier, John Adams, and Johann Galle. And interestingly, it was the first planet to be located via mathematical calculations!

Just like Uranus, it could be raining diamonds inside Neptune too! How cool is that?

NEPTUNE'S CHARACTERISTIC	VALUE
Mass (kilograms)	102×10^{24}
Approximate diameter (kilometres)	49.5×10^{3}
Escape velocity (kilometres/second)	23.5
Distance from the Sun (kilometres)	4515×10^{6}
Planet number from the Sun	8

Pluto

Discovered in 1930 by Clyde Tombaugh, Pluto is classified as a 'dwarf planet'. It was once considered the ninth planet in our solar system, but demoted due to its size and inability to clear and influence nearby asteroids and similar objects. =(

Located in the Kuiper Belt region of our solar system, it can get extremely cold here!

The average temperature on Pluto is -225°C (-373°F)!!! And it's pretty lonely. Luckily, Pluto has a moon named Charon to keep it company. =)

Unlike the other planets, Pluto orbits the Sun in an oval shaped path. This dwarf planet is unique!

PLUTO'S CHARACTERISTIC	VALUE
Mass (kilograms)	$0{\cdot}013 \times 10^{24}$
Approximate diameter (kilometres)	$2{\cdot}4 \times 10^{6}$
Escape velocity (kilometres/second)	1·3
Distance from the Sun (kilometres)	$5906{\cdot}4 \times 10^{6}$
Planet number from the Sun	(not classified anymore)

NASA's New Horizon spacecraft was the first spacecraft to fly up close to and picture Pluto!

Did you know that there is mathematical evidence to suggest another planet exits beyond Pluto?!

Scientists have called this hypothetical planet 'Planet X', and believe it orbits nearly 20 times further than Neptune!

The Sun

Perhaps the most important celestial body, responsible for our existence! Our Sun in all its mighty splendour shines everyday just so we can stay alive· We are extremely lucky to have it!

The Sun is considered a normal size star and is made up of mainly hydrogen and helium·

Hydrogen atoms fuse together inside the Sun to create helium· This process releases an incredible amount of energy that then travels through space and reaches us on earth· We feel this energy as heat and see it as light!

Did you know that the light from the Sun takes about eight minutes and 20 seconds to reach Earth?!

The ancient Egyptians worshiped their god Ra – the deity of the Sun!

THE SUN'S CHARACTERISTIC	VALUE
Mass (kilograms)	$1,988,400 \times 10^{24}$
Approximate diameter (kilometres)	$1{\cdot}4 \times 10^{6}$
Escape velocity (kilometres/second)	617·6

Did you know that these dark areas on the Sun's surface are cooler than the light areas? But they are still extremely hot!

The average temperature on the Sun reaches 5,500°C (9932°F) and about 15,000,000°C (27,000,000°F) inside the core!!!

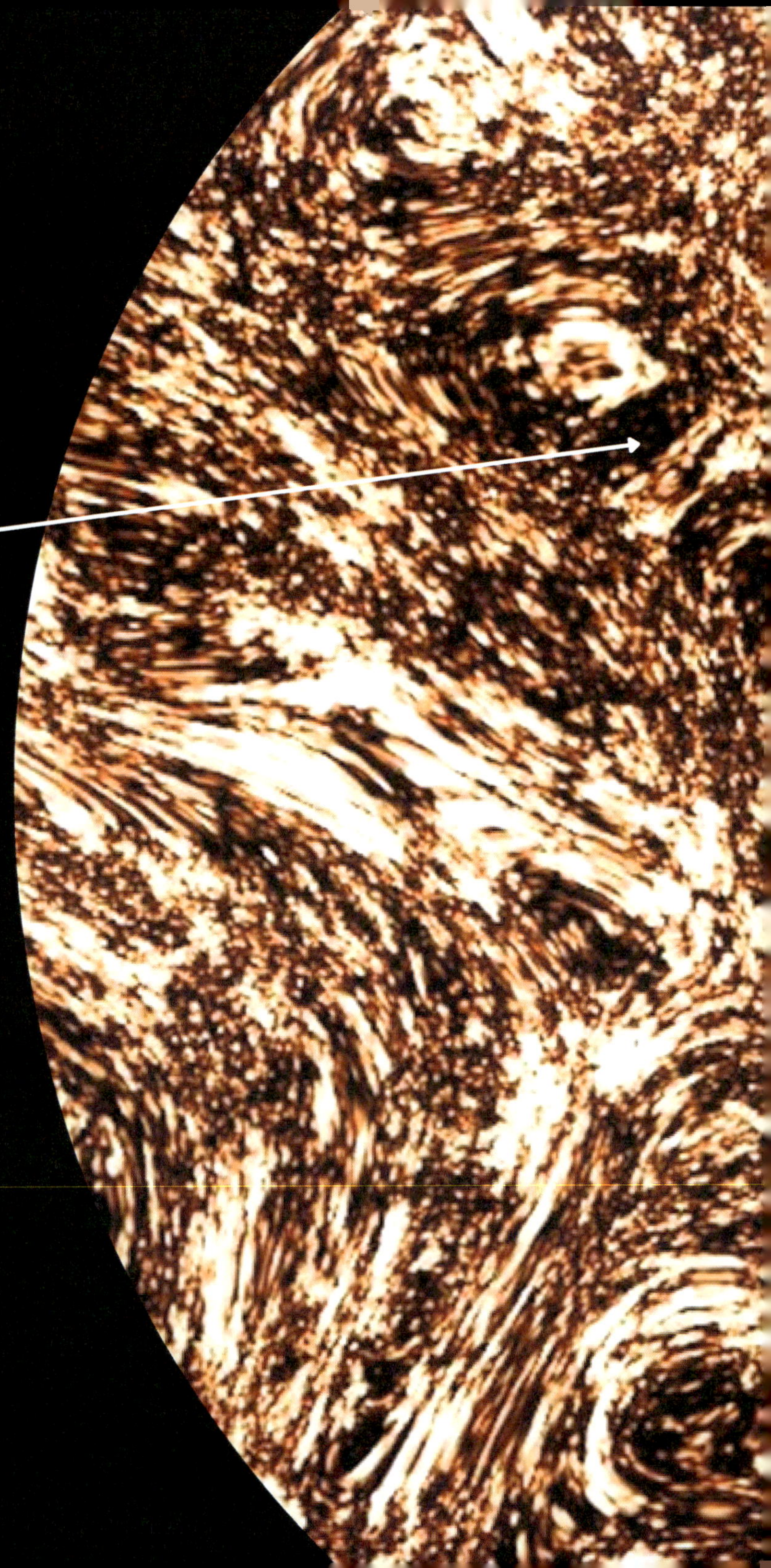

Solar flares happen all the time on the Sun and are a result of strong electromagnetic eruptions in the Sun's atmosphere. The intense energy particles from the flares travel to earth, interact with the magnetic fields, and create the most amazing light display in the north and south poles, known as the Aurora!

Solar Flares!

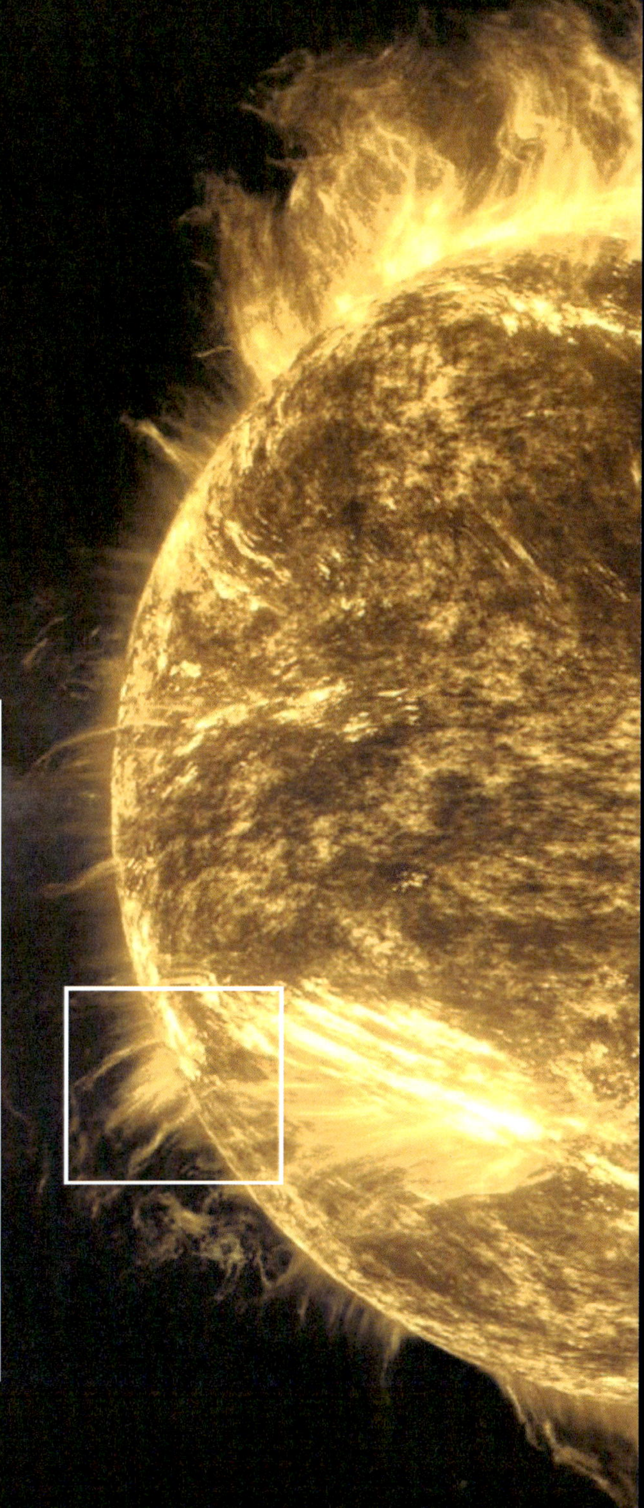

'Aurora Borealis' occurs in the northern hemisphere of Earth.

'Aurora Australis' occurs in the southern hemisphere of Earth.

Solar Eclipse

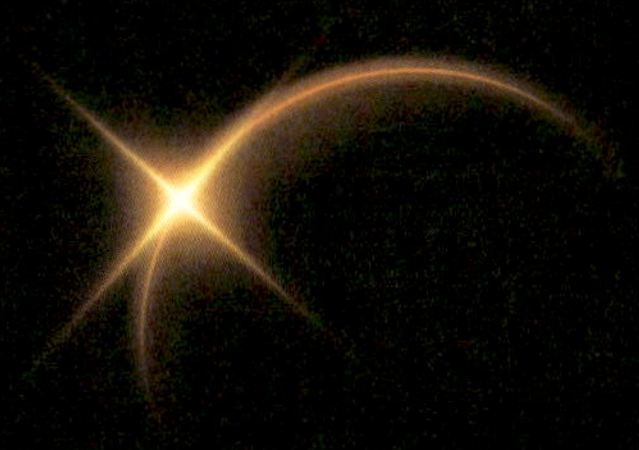

One of the most spectacular sights humans can experience on earth is the solar eclipse!

A solar eclipse is when the moon passes in front of the Sun and blocks out the light, partially or completely. A complete blocking of the Sun is called a 'total solar eclipse'. But the best part is that we can still see the Sun's outer atmosphere called 'corona' in all its detail!

The most famous scientist in human history, Albert Einstein, predicted that you can see stars that are behind the Sun! This is because of an amazing process called 'gravitational lensing', where the light from distant stars and objects can literally bend around the Sun because of its strong gravitational force!

Did you know that a total solar eclipse happens about every 1.5 years somewhere around the world?!

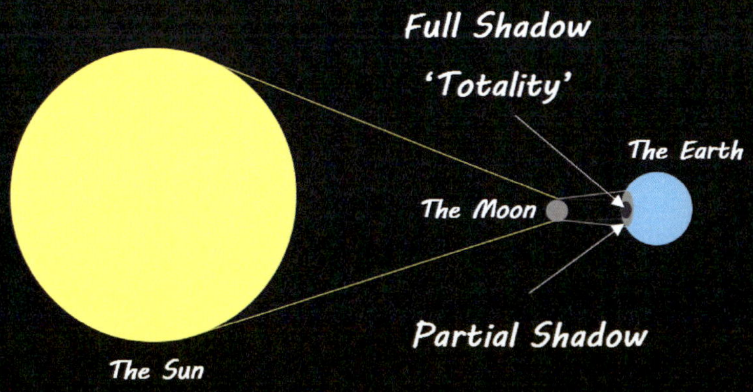

In our own galaxy called the Milky Way, there are billions of other stars! Some are 1000 times bigger or 100 times smaller than our Sun. They also vary in age. Some are older and some are much younger. But one thing is for sure, our Sun is the most impressive one to us!

NEXT STOP: INTERGALACTIC SPACE

The Milky Way

The Milky Way is a spiral galaxy with arms stretching out from the centre. Our solar system is in one of these arms, roughly halfway from the centre. It is called the Milky Way, because from Earth we can see a small band of light near the galactic centre that looks white like milk!

Our galaxy is about 100,000 light years across. That means it takes light about 100,000 years to get from one far side to the other!!!

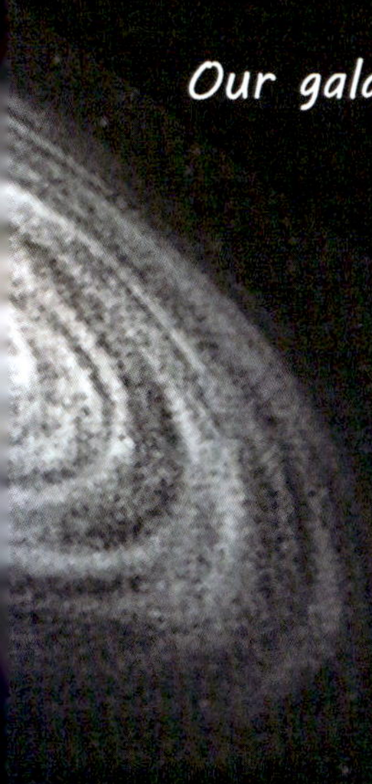

Did you know that ur closest neighbour galaxy is called Andromeda? It is located about 2.5 million light years from Earth!

It is estimated that there could be over two trillion galaxies in our universe!!!

Hope you are floating comfortably! There is still much more to see. As we travel through deep space, we will encounter even more strange worlds than we are used to. Our universe is filled with the most incredible objects that defy our understanding of the world around us.

Let us steer towards a part of the sky that I know is the place to go!

But first...

Did you like what we saw in our solar system? What amazed you?

My favourite planets are Earth, Saturn, and Jupiter. What are your favourite planets?

If you had to live on another planet, which would it be?

Remember there are no wrong answers to these questions! It's all part of the fun.

Nebula

A Nebula or Nebulae (more than one) is a giant intergalactic cloud of gases and dust that is usually created from the giant explosions of dying stars, called 'supernova'. It is also where new baby stars are being created.

The best thing about nebulae is that they are our universe's spectacular light show! They showcase their wonderful gaseous structures that are lit from the stars that are being born within them. I like to think of them as nature's canvas! The universe is painting new stars within them =).

The most famous nebulae that have been discovered are the Pillars of Creation, Eagle, Helix, Crab, Horsehead, Orion, Tarantula, and Lagoon nebula!

Did you know that the Hubble space telescope was used to discover the Pillars of Creation?

According to recorded text, the first observation of objects in a nebula was by the Alexandrian mathematician and scientist Ptolemy.

Pillars of Creation

Horsehead

Neutron Star

Look a Neutron Star!

These are one of the heaviest objects in our universe! Neutron stars are born after violent supernova.

Neutron stars are very small compared to our Sun, only about 15-30 kilometres across, but a single teaspoon of the star can weigh as much as one trillion kilograms!!! WOW!

Scientists typically use x-ray telescopes to find neutron stars, because these objects are difficult to see using optical telescopes but can emit x-ray radiation at centres of supernovas.

Did you know that neutron stars can spin? These are called 'pulsars', and they can even reach speeds of up to hundreds of rotations in a single second!!!

Did you know that when two neutron stars collide, it is called a 'kilonova'?!

Neutron Star

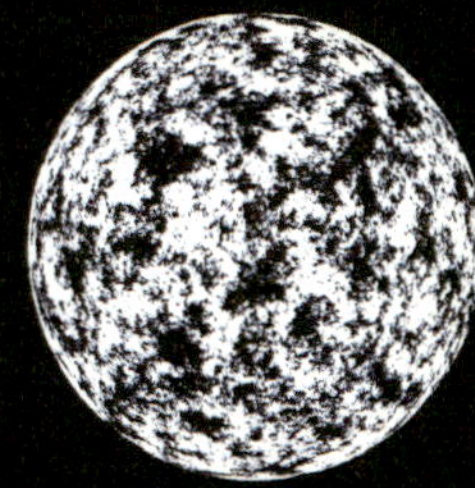

Some neutron stars emit incredible amounts of deadly radiation that shoot out as jets. These jets can measure millions of kilometres in length and travel at 1/3rd the speed of light!

Neutron stars are also known as the strongest magnets in our universe! This is because their magnetic fields can exceed billions and trillions that of Earth's!

There is even a type of neutron star called a 'magnetar'! These objects have magnetic fields thousands of times greater than a regular neutron star! What is even more crazy is that the magnetic fields can cause earthquakes on the surface of the star!

Did you know that many neutron stars in the universe travel through space as pairs?

These pairs are called 'binary systems' and are seen to orbit or 'dance' around each other, just like a pair of dancing ice skaters =).

Did you know that the Indian-American scientist Subrahmanyan Chandrasekhar discovered theories about the late evolution of massive stars?

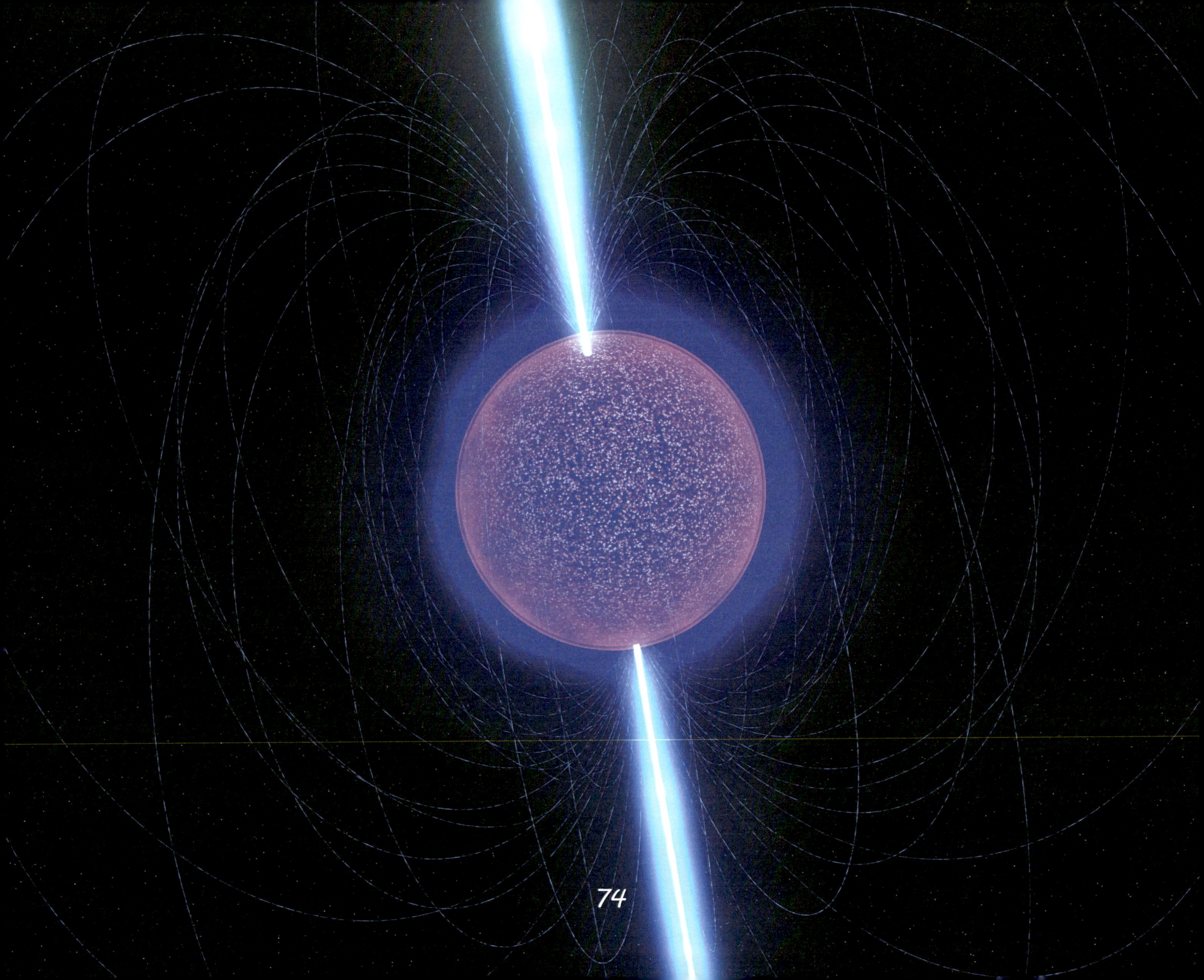

Hey...It's Leo again! I have an important message. We are about to witness one of the scariest objects ever seen in our universe!!!

Remember the neutron star? Well, this next object is even heavier, even bigger, and what's worse...we can't even see it! But don't worry, there's always a way!

Hold tight!

A Black Hole

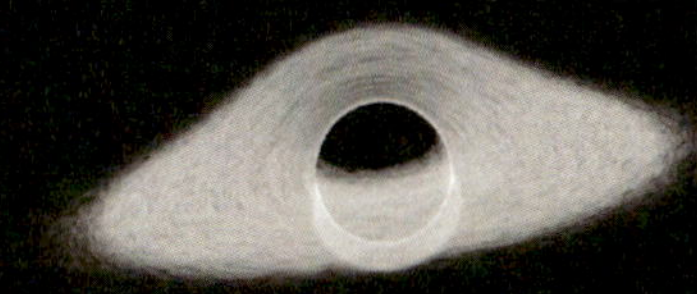

Black holes are one of the most silent and violent objects in our universe!

They are created when very big stars die in a violent supernova. During these explosions the star's nuclear energy is not enough to overcome its own immense gravitational force, and instead of turning into a neutron star, the star collapses in on itself! What is left is nothing but a huge and heavy 'hole' in space that sucks everything...even light!!! That is why we can't see black holes directly, but indirectly through light that is bent around it or orbiting it through something called an 'accretion disc'.

The point at which matter cannot escape the black hole's menacing pull is called the 'event horizon'.

Do not let these dark beasts scare you! Without them, our universe would be very different!

Did you know that at the centre of nearly every galaxy in the universe there is a supermassive black hole?!

A Black Hole

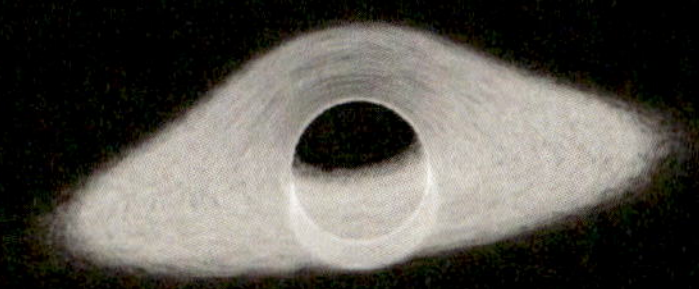

Black holes can be either stellar or supermassive. Steller black holes can weigh up to about 50 times the mass of our Sun, but supermassive black holes can weigh up to billions of times the mass of our Sun!!!

Nobody knows what lies at the centre of a black hole, but what we do know is that scientists call it the 'singularity'. It is the name given to a point in physics where the math simply 'breaks down' and we are left with unanswered questions!

You could be the next genius who will solve this puzzle!!!

Did you know that some scientists speculate that black holes may be the start of a new part of space or a portal to another universe?!

Did you know that in 2019 scientists released images of the first ever black hole?! This was one of the most impressive space discoveries in all human history!

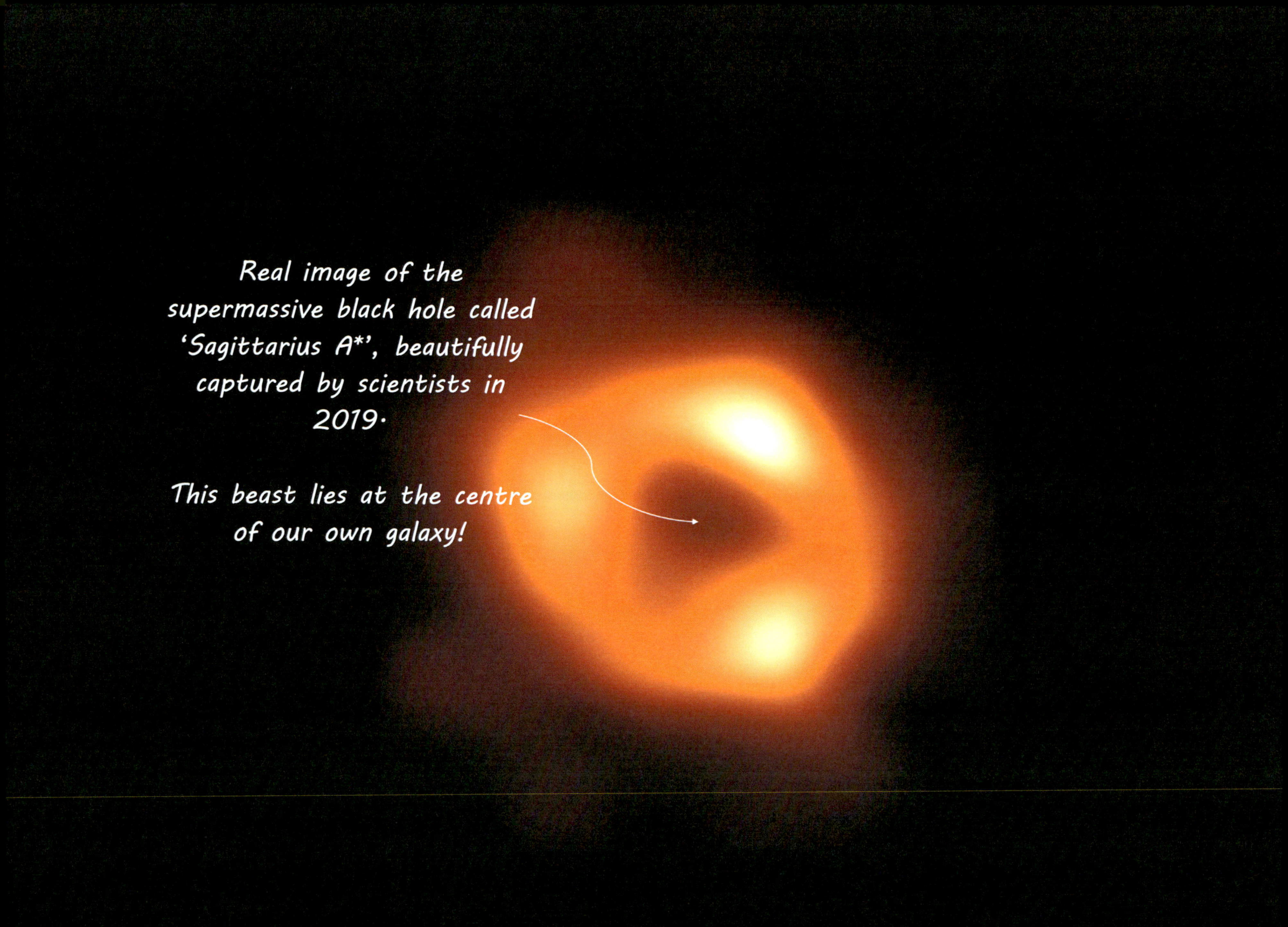

Real image of the supermassive black hole called 'Sagittarius A*', beautifully captured by scientists in 2019.

This beast lies at the centre of our own galaxy!

A Quasar! The most luminous object in the universe!

It is made up of a cloud of super-heated gases that surround a supermassive black hole.

This monster can release an extremely high energy jet of radiation and destroy anything in its path!

Pictured by the Hubble Space Telescope, this is an image of the quasar 3C 273 which is in an elliptical galaxy in the Virgo constellation!

Phew! We just managed to escape that black hole. That's what I call a close encounter!

Time to warp drive to another part of space and see colliding galaxies! But first, I know something that can help us. =)

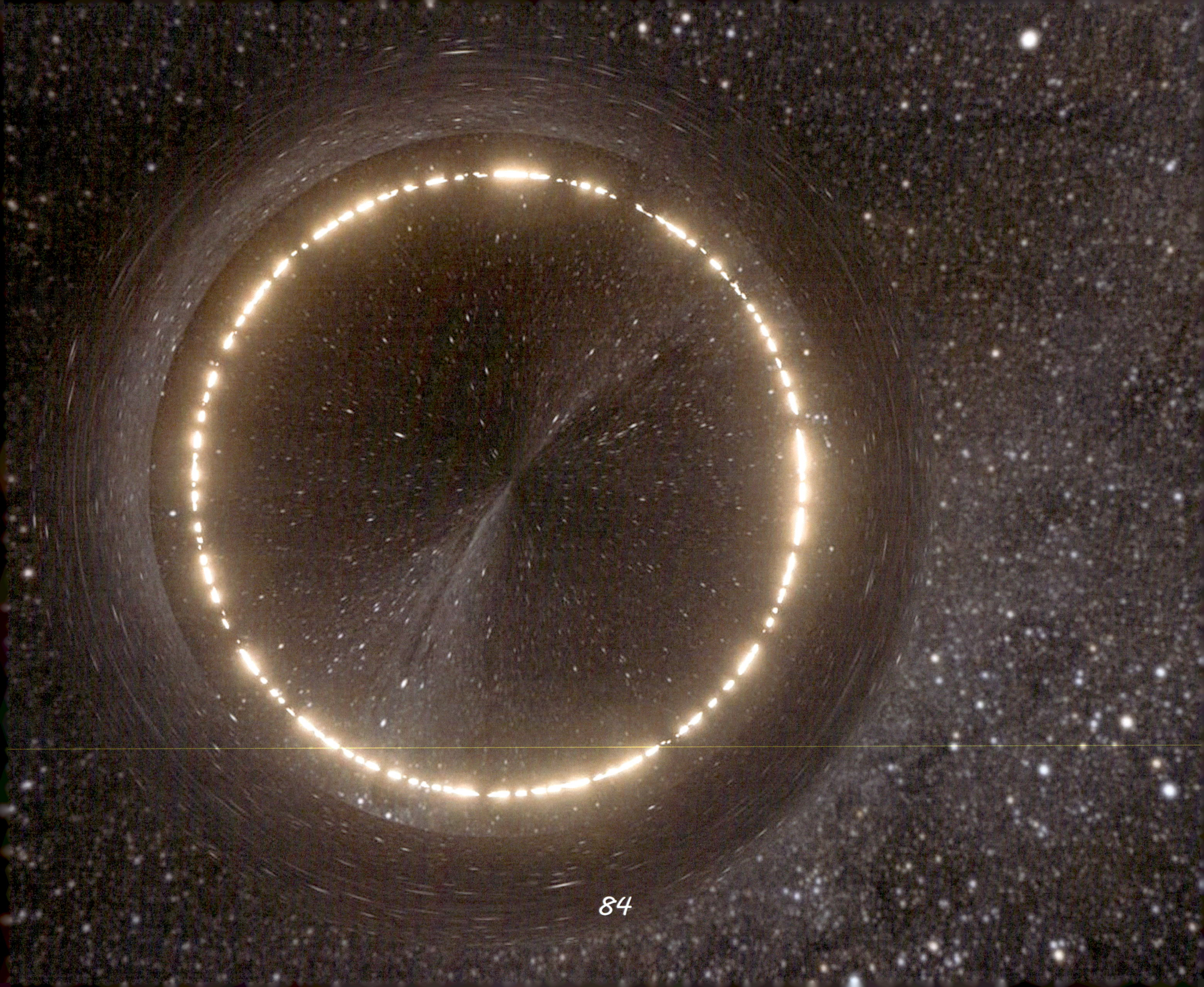

Wormholes

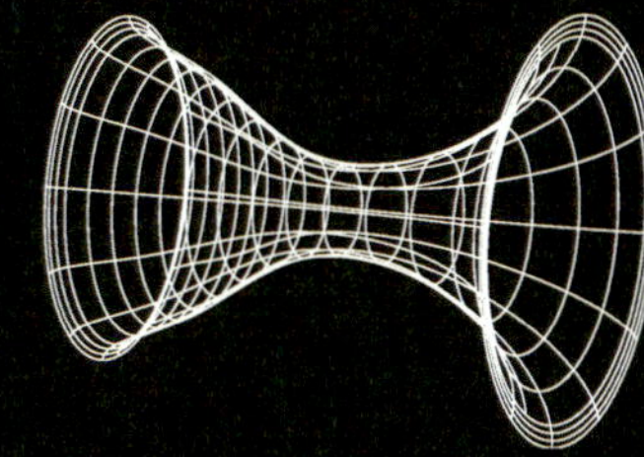

These highly mysterious objects have never been seen before! They are 'theoretical' objects that connect two different points in space and time, just like a tunnel!

They were first predicted by Einstein's general theory of relativity!

A wormhole can allow anything that goes through it to quickly travel across vast distances in no time! This could be a few meters to travelling across the entire universe!

That means time travel may be possible, just like in the movies! =)

Did you know scientists think that there may be different types of wormholes?!

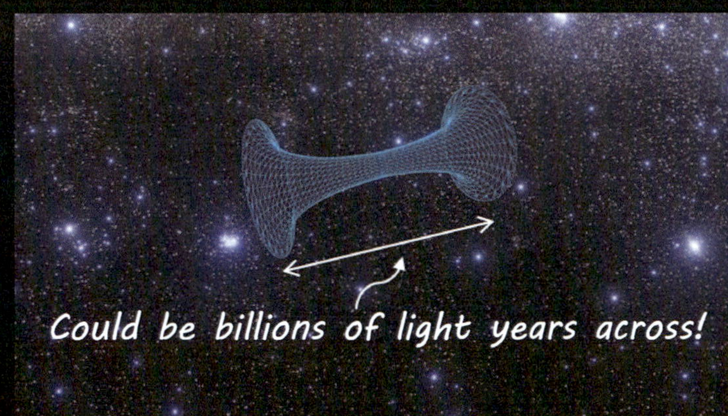

Colliding Galaxies

Galaxies across the universe can collide with one another in a spectacular display of gravitational attraction!

The result of collisions can cause the galaxies to form into a much larger single galaxy, or all the galaxies can be ripped apart!

This process can take an exceptionally long time, and solar systems inside the galaxies can even be flung out into deep space!

Scientists can now create amazing realistic simulations of colliding galaxies on their computers! Using realistic physics principles, they can even predict what will happen when more than one galaxy collides!

Did you know that it is predicted that our Milky Way galaxy will one day collide with our neighbour, the Andromeda galaxy?!

But don't worry, this is expected to happen in another four billion years! Phew.

Pictured by the Hubble Space Telescope, this is an image of the galaxy NGC 2623 located about 250 million light years away! It is a result of two galaxies that once collided and merged with each other!

Look! We've found something called an 'Exoplanet'! It's even orbiting its neighbour gas giant. Cool beans!

I can see the planet has a solid surface and a very thin atmosphere! But looking at my data it says it's really cold...about -120°C (-184°F)! The gas giant is filled with a mixture of nitrogen, oxygen, silicate droplets, methane, carbon dioxide, and hydrogen. Winds are strong there too!

Exoplanets

An exoplanet is any planet that lies outside our own solar system.

They can belong to their own solar system or even float gently in space on their own. Planets that are not part of a solar system are called 'rogue planets'.

It is estimated that there is at least one planet for every star in our own galaxy. These planets vary in size, temperature, composition, and orbits.

Did you know scientists have discovered many exoplanets within our own milky way galaxy?!

They even believe that some of them may have just the right conditions to contain certain types of life forms!

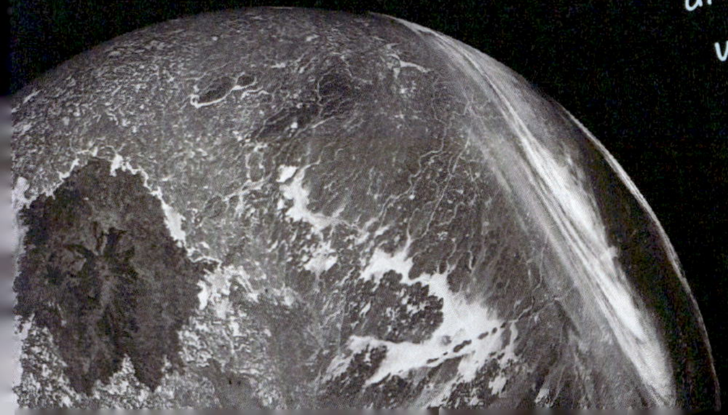

Exoplanets

There are currently five ways of discovering exoplanets? Two of the most common are:

1) Measuring if a star 'wobbles' slightly because of a nearby planet's gravity.

2) The second is by using telescopes to see if a planet moves across a star. Known as 'transiting', this method relies on seeing a small drop in a star's light because it is being blocked by the planet.

What do you think could be lying on some exoplanets?

If you could live on an exoplanet of your choice, what would you want it to look like? And what important resources do you think would be necessary to keep you alive?

Oh wow! I've always wanted to see one of these next objects. It's a Red Supergiant star! And it looks like a small planet of some kind is travelling in front of it.

Shortly after, we'll see even more red giants amongst some interesting parts of the sky.

Red Supergiant

A red supergiant is a dying star! It gets its name from hydrogen fusing in the outer layers, which as they cool give off its red colour. These are the largest stars in our universe, in terms of volume!

Although these are the largest stars in the universe, they are not the heaviest, brightest, or the hottest!

A single red supergiant can shine as bright as a million Suns!

The brightest star we can see from Earth is called 'Sirius', derived from the Greek word to mean glowing. Even our ancient ancestors saw this star!

You can see Sirius near the constellation Orion. Next time on a clear night, look up to find it!

Star Clusters

These clusters are a collection of various old and new stars which are gravitationally held together.

Groups that mainly have thousands or millions of old stars are considered 'globular clusters', while those with only a few hundred or so baby stars are considered 'open clusters'. Open clusters also form in gas clouds – just like what we see in nebulae!

There are a variety of stars ranging in mass, brightness (luminosity), and size. Some are red giants, while others are in their 'main sequence', or 'white dwarf' stars.

Globular clusters form with little gas clouds around, indicating that these must be very old stars, and not many new stars are being born.

Did you know that our Sun is expected to turn into a white dwarf when it dies?! Once a white dwarf, the star will slowly cool off into lower and lower temperatures!

Perhaps there will be no evidence that our Sun once hosted the greatest life form in our universe! =(

I think we may have found something beyond our wildest dreams. A habitable planet!

This one has two moons, and four neighbouring stars close by too!

Let's check it out.

Where do you think the other star is?

Hint: we can see the light side of this planet and its moon! =)

Habitable Zone

The habitable zone is an area within a solar system where the conditions are just right for liquid water to form. Another name for a habitable zone is the 'goldilocks zone'. Because it is just perfect. Not too hot, and not too cold.

Scientists expect that within these conditions there is a high probability that life forms can exist!

Our planet, Earth, is within a goldilocks zone.

It is also important that the host star of a solar system's habitable zone be stable, and not too big or too small. Just like our own Sun! =)

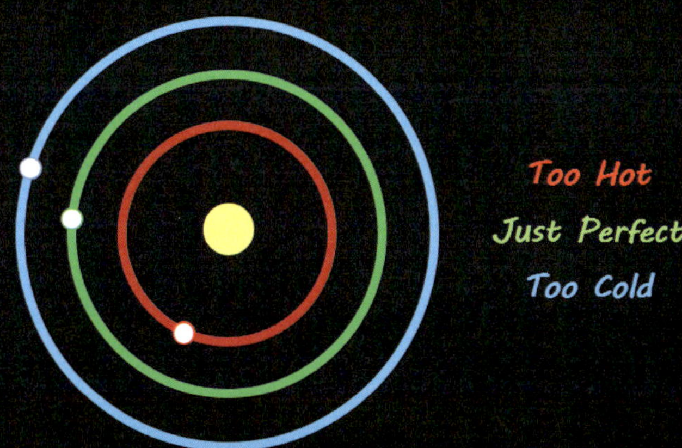

Imagine what's out there!

I sense some dark mysterious force around us!

These galaxies are moving in ways that shouldn't be possible!

What might it be?

Dark Matter

All the observable objects in the universe are made up of 'matter'. This ordinary matter is any substance that has both volume and mass.

When scientists look at the data and images of space, they find something really strange. It turns out that galaxies and stars are moving in weird patterns than what should be allowed by ordinary matter! Also, they find that clusters of galaxies are being held together by some mysterious unseen 'stuff'.

They term this unseen stuff as 'dark matter'! A kind of substance that does not emit, reflect, or absorb light, but its influence seems to be huge on the entire observable universe!

Did you know that it is estimated that 27% of the universe is made of dark matter!!!

What do you think dark matter is?

Dark Energy

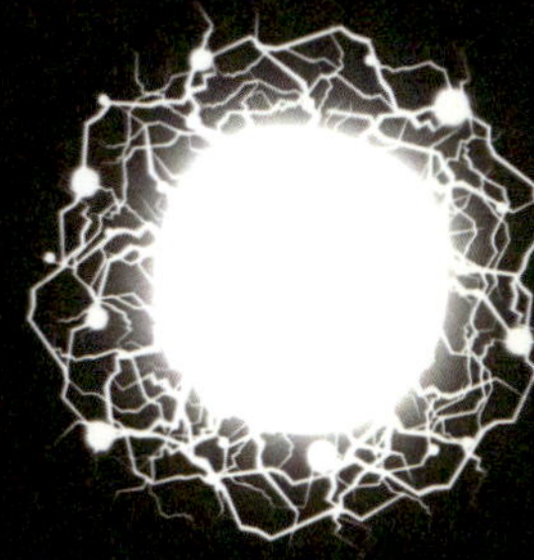

Even more strange than dark matter, is something called 'dark energy'!

Scientists reckon that about 68%-70% of the universe is made up of this force.

The concept of dark energy, or this invisible force, was first theorized by Albert Einstein, and observed when scientists saw that galaxies were moving apart faster and faster! This repulsion force is making the universe accelerate, stretch, and making new space! What's even crazy is the further out we see, the faster the universe is moving!

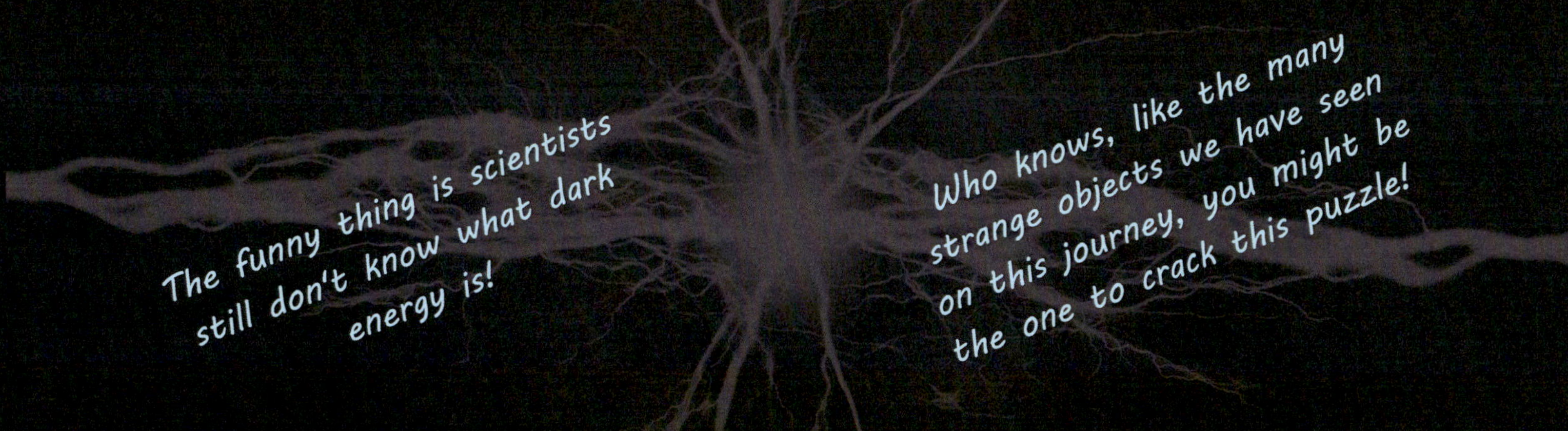

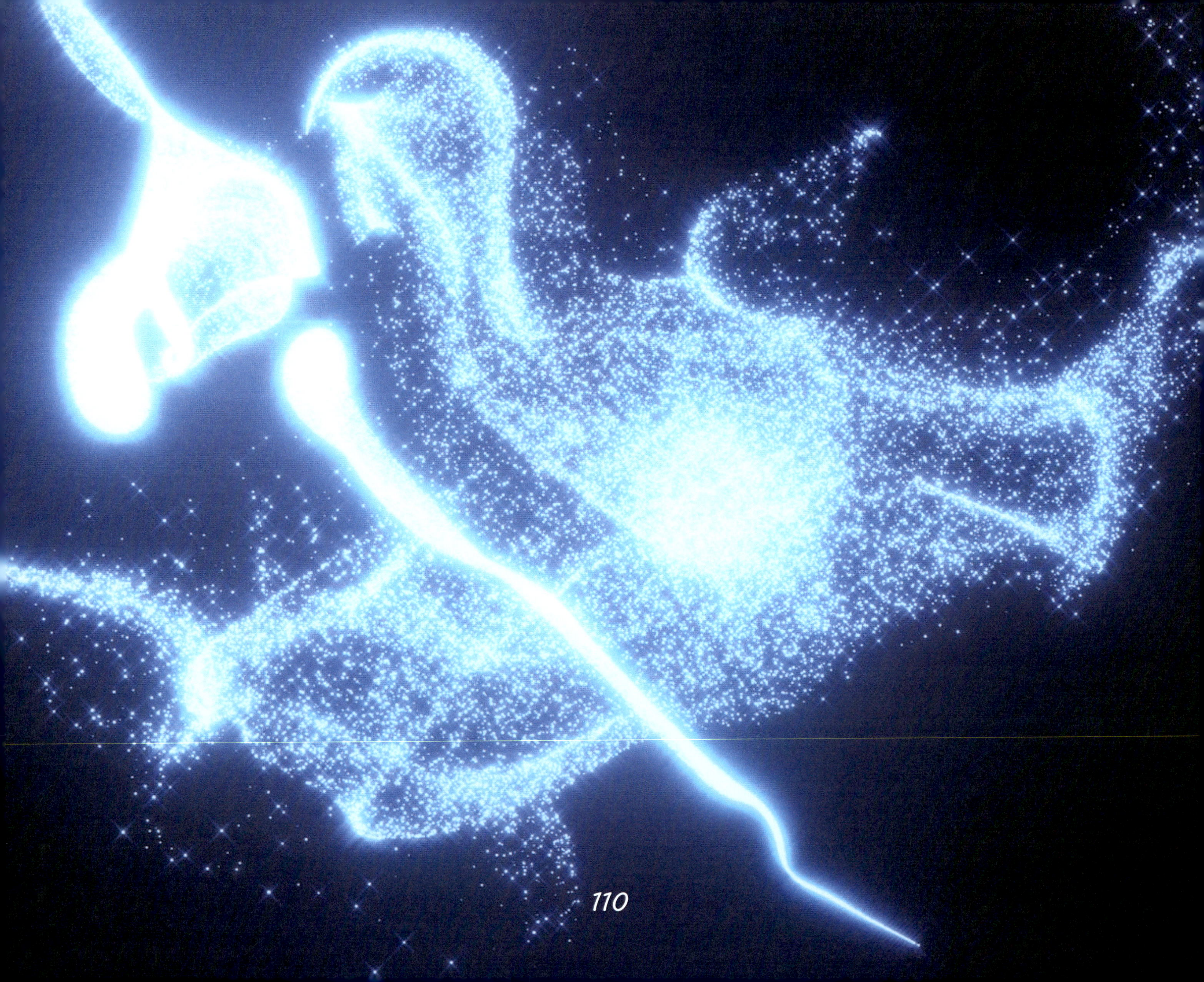

Light

One of the most important aspects of our universe is light!

Light is a form of electromagnetic radiation that we humans can see with our eyes, and it is made up of tiny subatomic particles called 'photons'. Photons do not have any mass but carry energy! This energy is partly responsible for our lives!

Light can be scattered through different materials, allowing us to see all the colours of the rainbow!

Weirdly, light can behave as both a wave and a particle! This confused scientists for a long time and is still a fun but mysterious topic for many!

Did you know that scientists managed to slow down light to about 61 kilometres per hour in a lab? Cool!

The speed of light in a vacuum is about one billion kilometres per hour!!! But the speed of light can change depending on the material it travels through!

Hey…we're nearing the end of our journey now, but there's just a few spectacular sights I have lined up on our route!

Oh WOW! Looks like we might be passing by an advanced civilization, and they've managed to build one of the most impressive engineering structures ever - a Dyson Sphere!!!

Dyson Sphere

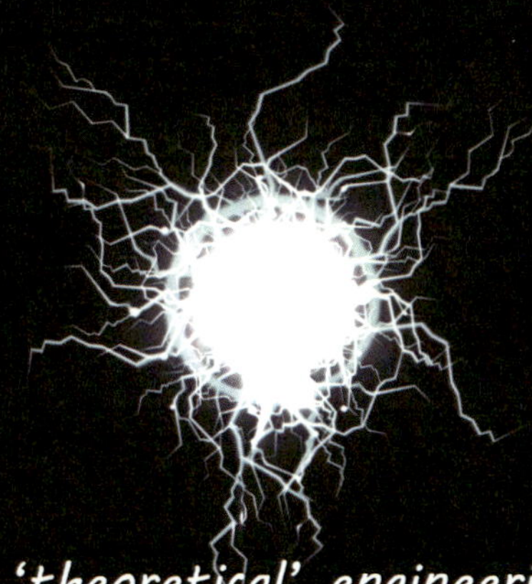

Named after the famous scientist, Freeman Dyson, a Dyson sphere is a 'theoretical' engineering structure that surrounds a star and captures its solar energy. This energy can then be used for a practical purpose, such as providing power to run a planet's cities and machines.

These space megastructures are only created by highly advanced species who have the resources and materials to do so!

The white modules you see around the star, which make up the Dyson sphere, are the machines that capture and convert the solar energy. These machines can be operated like 'drones' and be controlled to move around the star.

If you could design a Dyson sphere, what would it look like? And how would it work?

What would you use a Dyson sphere for?

Binary Stars

A binary system of stars is a pair of stars (two) that are gravitationally bound to each other. The stars orbit around a single point called the 'centre of mass'. Just like the neutron stars orbiting around each other. Because of the strong gravitational forces, the stars can deform and look slightly warped.

You can find multiple star systems in the universe where there are more than two stars gravitationally bound to each other!

Blue stars are much hotter than red coloured stars!

It is estimated that about 85% of stars are binary pair systems!...

...That means our own Sun is a very special star!

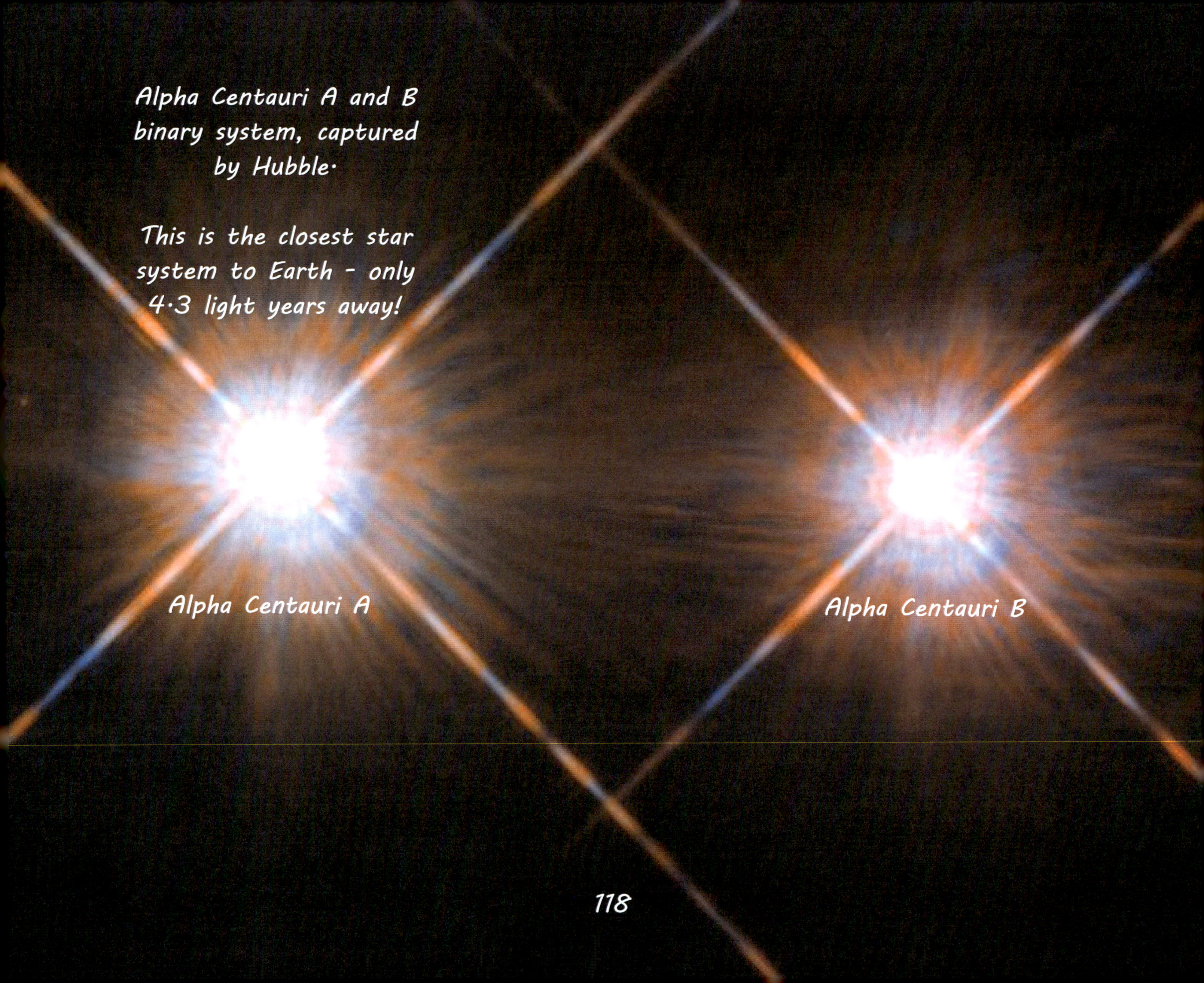

Alpha Centauri A and B binary system, captured by Hubble.

This is the closest star system to Earth - only 4.3 light years away!

WHOA! We're nearing a supermassive black hole again!

This time it's swallowing a whole star alive!

Black Hole Eating a Star

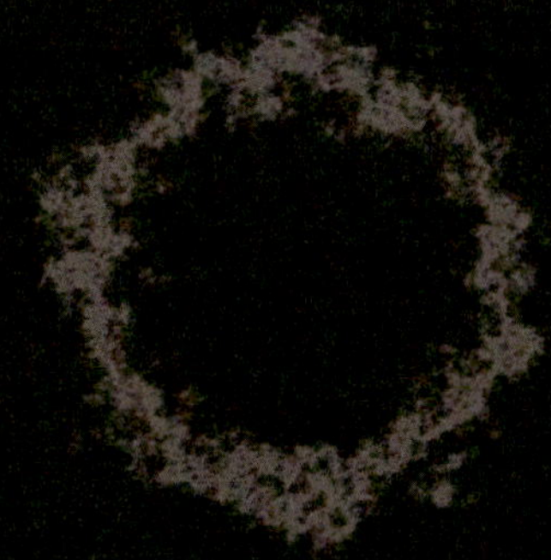

As stars get close to supermassive black holes their mass starts to be ripped apart from the strong tidal forces of the black hole!

While the black hole devours a star, the debris from the collision creates the accretion disc of stellar mass. This disc is filled with luminous matter from the star and can be seen from light years away!

During the star's death, strong electromagnetic radiation in the form of X-rays and UV rays can be detected using instruments, while the visible light can be seen with the naked eye.

But not all the matter that falls into a black hole may disappear!

he famous scientist Stephen Hawking discovered a theoretical idea that black holes emit particles into space, called 'Hawking Radiation'!

That means even black holes in the long distant future can die!

We could be staring into a portal to a new universe!

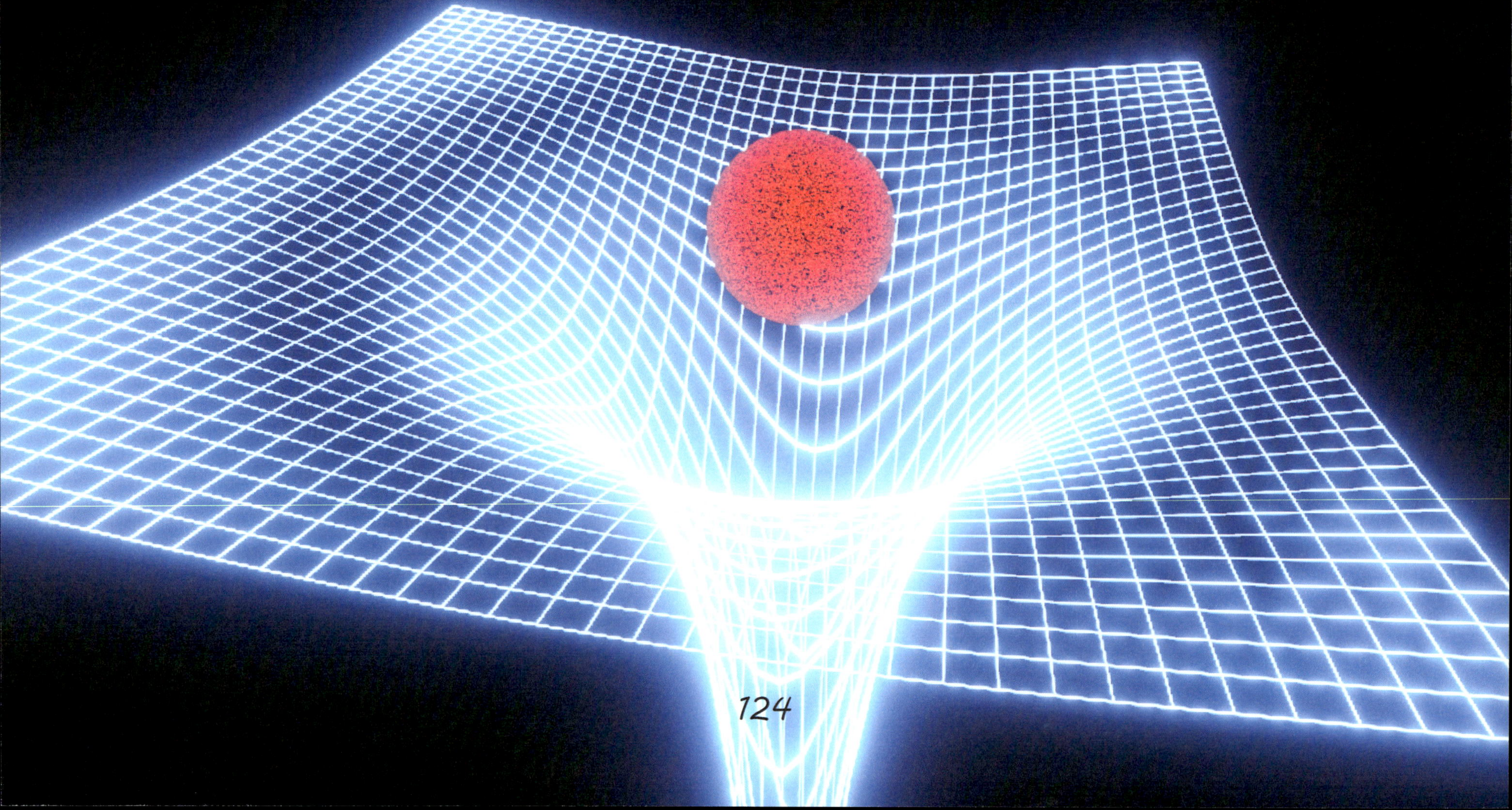

The Fabric of Spacetime

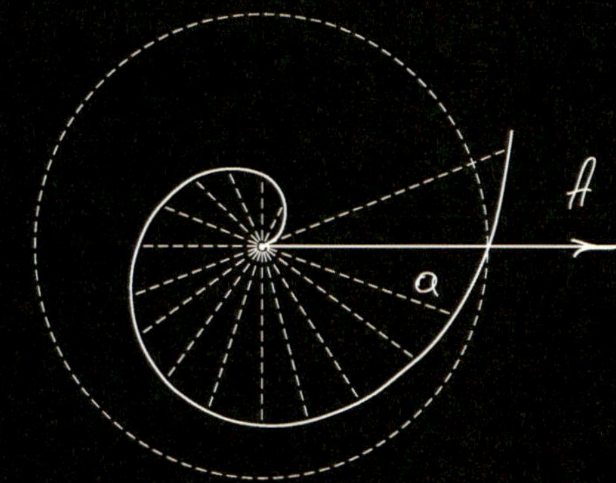

The Spacetime fabric is a theoretical concept that allows us to understand and visualise how the force of gravity works across the universe.

It was created by Albert Einstein, who saw space as a 'fabric' or sheet that could be bent, stretched, and warped in the presence of matter and energy.

Einstein's famous theory of general relativity says that the presence of matter causes space to curve, and the curvature of space tells matter how to move! =) This is the concept of 'gravity', and why the presence of a star or planet 'warps' spacetime which causes nearby matter, such as a moon, to travel in a curved path around it. We call this motion an 'orbit'!

The heavier the object, the bigger the spacetime warping. =)

Did you know that scientists think the spacetime fabric can ripple just like the ripples in a pond?!

These ripples are known as gravitational waves, and scientists are working to measure them!

All matter, such as a star, warps the spacetime fabric in all directions of space!

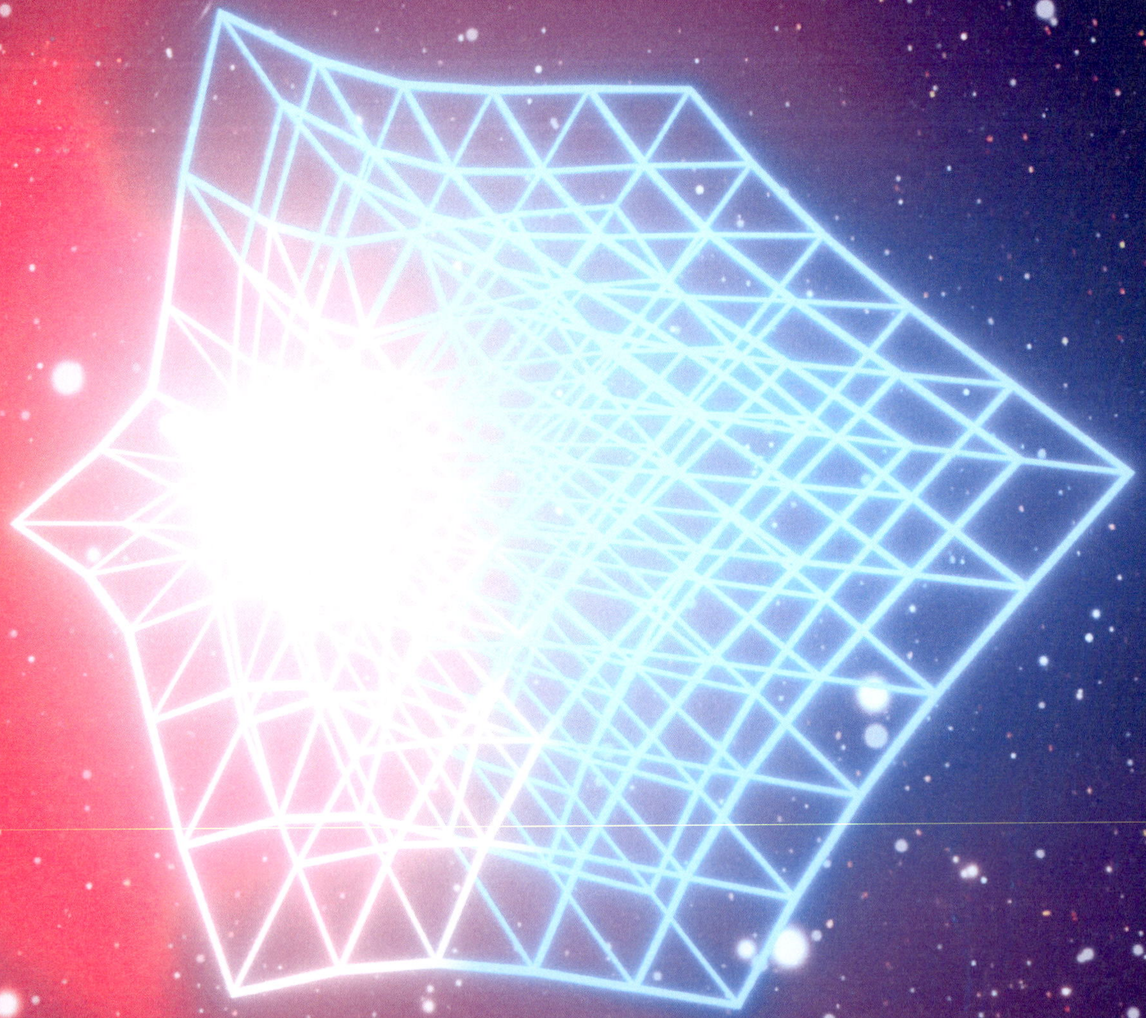

The Fabric of Spacetime

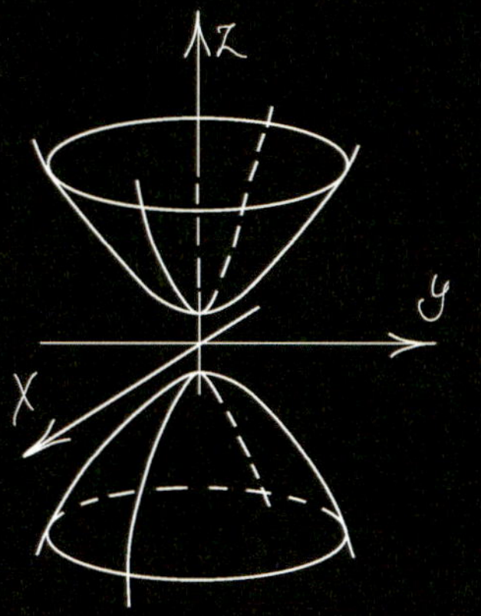

It is called spacetime because the concept brings together the three dimensions of space and the fourth dimension of time! This means that time too can change depending on how warped spacetime becomes!!! If we had passed through the event horizon when we flew by that supermassive black hole, time would have looked like it stood still for us by anyone looking at us from the outside! This just simply boggles the mind!

The coolest thing about this concept is that it has passed all the real-life experiments conducted! Scientists have been able to accurately predict how planets, stars, black holes, and other objects behave in space! Awesome!

Did you know that the first experiments to prove Einstein's theory of gravity correct involved seeing star light bent around the Sun during a solar eclipse?!

What an incredible journey, and time to be alive! We're so lucky to be able to witness the marvels in our universe!

There aren't many people who know what you know now! And who knows, you might be on the path to discover even more incredible things!

I think it's time to warp drive back home using another wormhole!

Back to where we belong…
Earth

Welcome Home!

Whenever you're outside,
look up and around at your world.
Feel the breeze running around you,
and the Earth beneath your feet.
Hear the sounds of everyday life,
including your inner heartbeat.

What a trip! I really hope you enjoyed your journey! And remember, it doesn't stop here! Now that your back home safe and sound, I provided some fun puzzles to try!

Until next time, keep exploring!

Rock on!

PUZZLES

I	U	I	N	O	U	M	A	R	S	U	P	E	E
R	R	N	S	R	M	E	R	C	U	R	Y	N	R
U	M	O	P	B	I	E	T	I	O	A	T	B	R
N	O	T	P	I	O	A	N	N	O	N	L	J	N
T	O	O	R	T	R	R	M	E	A	U	E	U	R
A	N	U	E	T	R	T	R	N	B	S	B	P	U
R	T	S	U	U	S	H	H	P	O	S	D	I	T
N	A	R	N	R	L	S	U	P	R	S	I	T	A
Y	U	P	L	U	T	O	N	L	L	B	O	E	S
U	R	S	A	T	R	S	U	N	E	V	R	R	E
C	E	U	H	K	U	I	P	E	R	B	E	L	T
N	E	P	T	U	N	E	V	U	P	O	T	N	N
T	R	A	R	N	I	T	R	E	S	E	S	A	I
N	E	N	A	S	A	S	U	I	T	R	A	R	U

WORD SEARCH I

How many words can you find?

ASTEROIDBELT
PLUTO
VENUS
NEPTUNE
ORBIT
MARS
MERCURY
SATURN
MOON
SUN
JUPTIER
URANUS
KUIPERBELT
EARTH

Rules:
Words can appear horizontally, vertically, and diagonally in any direction.

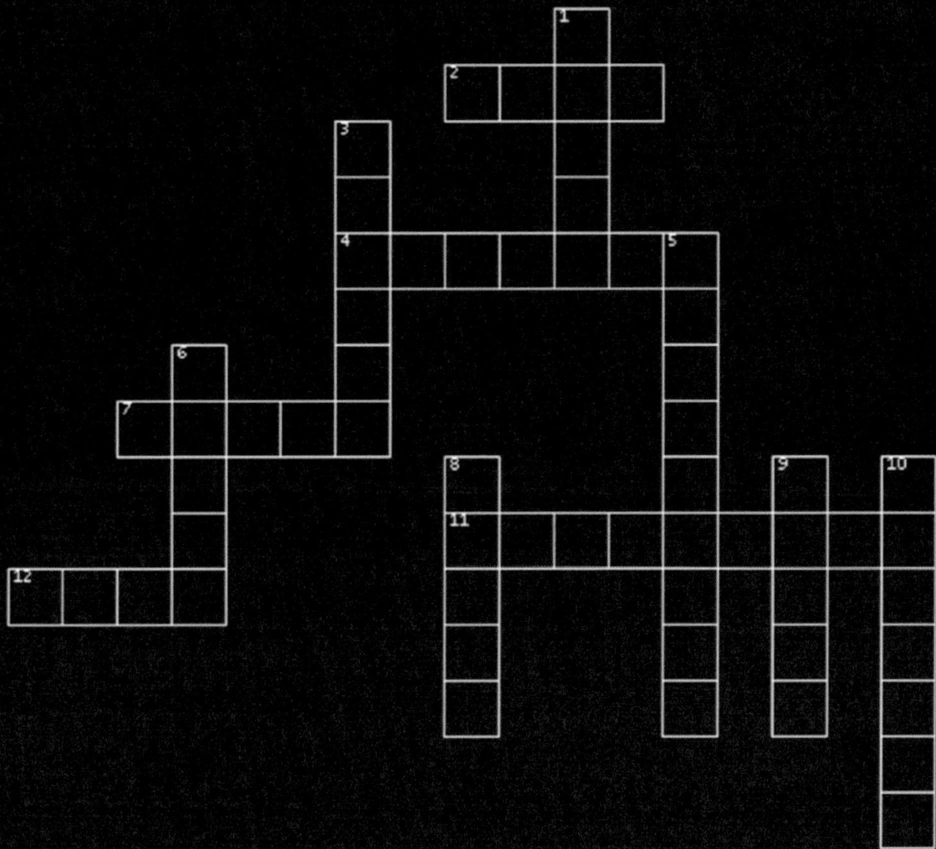

CROSSWORD

How many words can you find, using the clues below?

ACROSS

2. A natural satellite
4. A group of stars
7. A curved path taken by an object in space
11. The distance travelled by light
12. The red planet

DOWN

1. A small icy object that heats up as it nears a star
3. A machine designed to take people into space
5. Transmission of energy
6. A form of high energy electromagnetic radiation
8. A dwarf planet that was once our 9th planet
9. The hottest planet in our solar system
10. A force that keeps us on the ground

WORD SEARCH II

How many words can you find?

E	M	P	I	B	L	A	C	K	H	O	L	E	A
G	O	N	M	E	L	M	Y	N	E	U	N	Y	I
S	T	T	E	Q	A	N	L	E	P	M	O	C	P
T	A	N	U	U	A	A	O	B	O	I	T	G	I
H	M	A	A	A	T	Y	E	U	C	L	O	A	R
A	K	I	T	S	T	R	H	L	S	K	H	L	R
A	N	G	E	A	E	R	O	A	E	Y	P	A	A
A	O	D	M	R	O	N	C	N	L	W	M	X	S
W	E	E	R	P	P	A	E	H	E	A	T	Y	S
E	C	R	N	O	P	L	S	R	T	Y	E	N	L
R	C	C	S	Y	M	R	I	H	G	O	U	G	R
A	L	C	P	T	N	E	G	O	T	Y	X	C	Y
E	A	O	Y	E	A	I	D	H	U	E	C	E	A
S	P	A	C	E	L	R	I	A	D	U	C	T	T

STAR
ATOM
QUASAR
TELESCOPE
ANDROMEDA
MILKYWAY
SPACE
PHOTON
BLACKHOLE
ENERGY
NEBULA
LIGHT
NEUTRON
REDGIANT
GALAXY

Rules:
Words can appear horizontally, vertically, and diagonally in any direction.

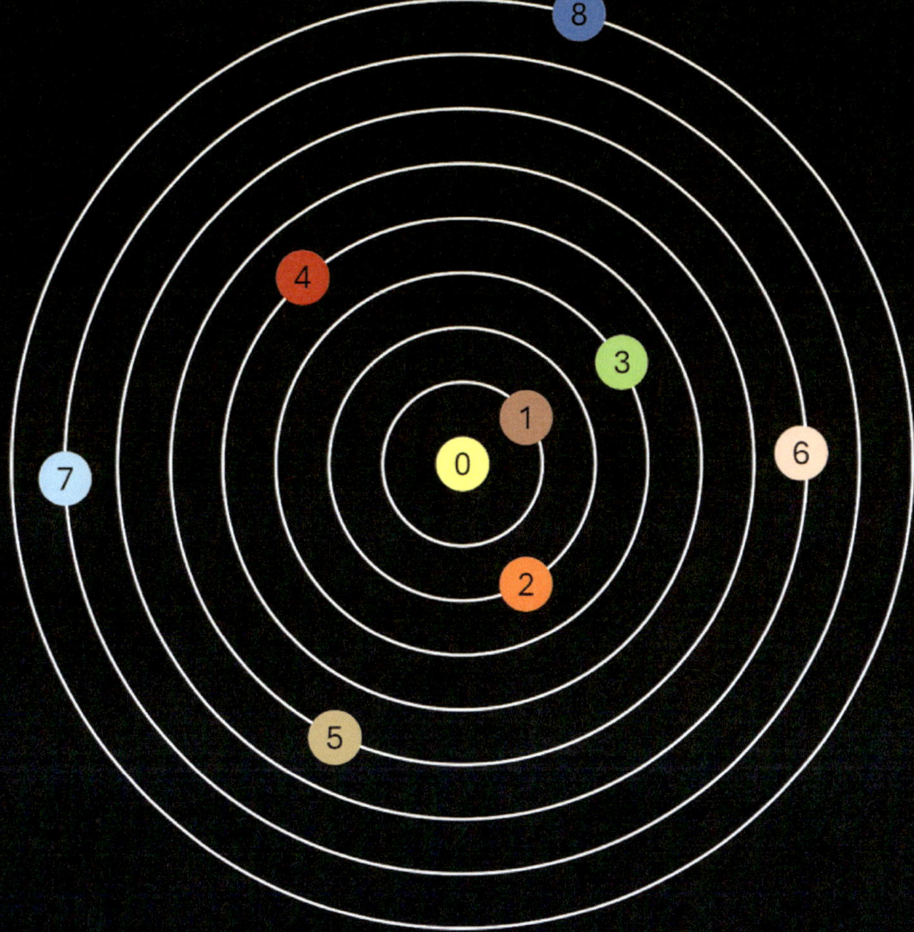

OUR SOLAR SYSTEM

How many celestial objects and planets can you identify?

0. ______________________________
1. ______________________________
2. ______________________________
3. ______________________________
4. ______________________________
5. ______________________________
6. ______________________________
7. ______________________________
8. ______________________________

WORD SEARCH III

How many words can you find?

P	W	E	T	E	N	A	L	P	O	X	E	N	G
B	A	P	E	U	I	L	E	H	U	B	B	L	E
I	N	B	R	A	E	G	I	L	G	N	E	W	N
G	A	E	U	N	I	V	E	R	S	E	N	E	E
B	V	E	S	Y	E	O	O	N	M	O	G	W	E
A	O	I	G	N	I	E	O	I	I	O	S	O	I
N	N	N	E	N	V	E	T	T	I	L	G	R	N
G	R	E	M	I	H	E	A	B	H	Y	G	M	S
S	E	B	L	U	C	I	O	G	G	T	N	H	T
N	P	N	E	A	D	R	O	D	E	I	I	O	E
N	U	I	P	A	C	R	U	L	T	V	K	L	I
M	S	S	R	E	G	P	I	A	V	A	W	E	N
I	P	A	R	T	I	C	L	E	P	R	A	I	Y
N	T	U	A	O	P	N	I	R	H	G	H	N	N

RADIATION
LENSING
UNIVERSE
GRAVITY
WORMHOLE
PARTICLE
BIGBANG
EXOPLANET
HUBBLE
HAWKING
SUPERNOVA
SPACETIME
EINSTEIN

Rules:
Words can appear horizontally, vertically, and diagonally in any direction.

Neutron Star | The Moon | Red Supergiant | Jupiter | Black Hole

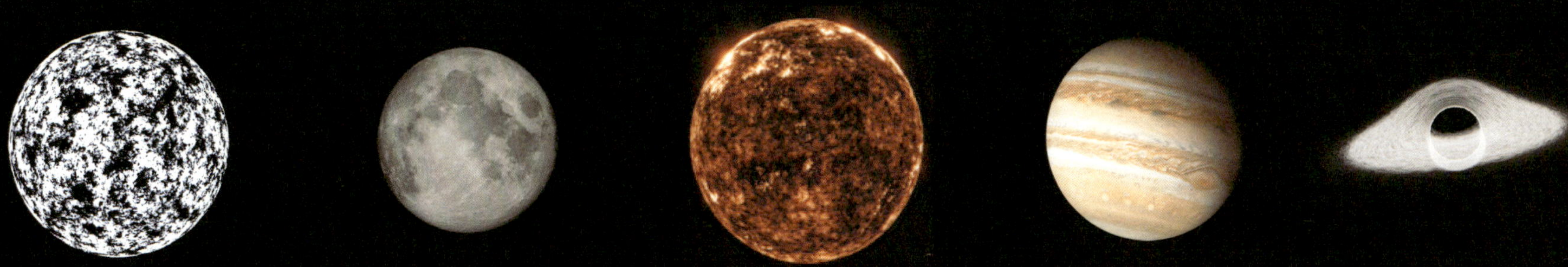

1. | 2. | 3. | 4. | 5.

SPACETIME

Match the object with the correct warping effect on spacetime.

1. ______________________________

2. ______________________________

3. ______________________________

4. ______________________________

5. ______________________________

RIDDLES

1· I am sometimes full but never spill· I even have a dark side· What am I?

2· I twinkle, but I'm not an eye· What am I?

3· I attract but cannot be seen, and I eat everything even a light beam· What am I?

4· People use me to measure heat, and I get a front seat to view the Sun· What am I?

5· I protect the solar system with all my size, and I have a scar that is visible from earth· What am I?

6· No one likes me because I am the universe's speed limit, but I am the reason to make you see· What am I?

7· I am the result of a star's death, but I give birth to new stars· What am I?

8· You make me during the day but use me during the night, just to see those objects that shine so bright· What am I?

9· With a kiss I seem to stop, but nothing can outrun me, and I am the 4th dimension of the theory of relativity· What am I?

10· You can fly into me, and I am all around you· What am I?

ANSWERS

WORD SEARCH I, II, and III

Did you manage to find all the words?
The answers are all in the puzzle! =)
Take your time to look carefully.

CROSSWORD

Across: 2. Moon 4. Cluster 7. Orbit 11. Lightyear 12. Mars

Down: 1. Comet 3. Rocket 5. Radiation 6. XRays 8. Pluto 9. Venus 10. Gravity

OUR SOLAR SYSTEM

0. The Sun
1. Mercury
2. Venus
3. Earth
4. Mars
5. Jupiter
6. Saturn
7. Uranus
8. Neptune

SPACETIME

1. Black Hole
2. Jupiter
3. The Moon
4. Neutron Star
5. Red Supergiant

RIDDLES

1. The Moon
2. A Star
3. Black Hole
4. Mercury
5. Jupiter
6. Light
7. Supernova
8. Telescope
9. Time
10. Space

Image Credits

The Author would like to sincerely thank and acknowledge the following

- Galaxy Cluster MACSJ0717.5+3745 (pg 16): NASA, ESA, and the HST Frontier Fields Team (STSci), https://esahubble.org/
- Butterfly Nebula (pg 17): NASA, ESA, and the Hubble SM4 ERO Team, https://esahubble.org/
- Galaxy NCG 1316 (pg 18): NASA, ESA and the Hubble Heritage Team (STScI/AURA), https://esahubble.org/
- Pillars of creation image (pg 68): NASA, ESA and the Hubble Heritage Team (STScI/AURA), https://esahubble.org/
- Horsehead Nebula (pg 69): NASA, ESA and the Hubble Heritage Team (AURA/STScI), https://esahubble.org/
- Sagittarius A* (pg 80): EHT Collaboration, https://eventhorizontelescope.org/
- Quasar 3C 273 (pg 82): ESA/Hubble & NASA, https://esahubble.org/
- Galaxy merger NGC 2623 (pg 88): ESA/Hubble & NASA, https://esahubble.org/
- Globular cluster NGC 3201 (pg 98): ESA/Hubble & NASA, https://esahubble.org/
- Alpha Centauri binary system (pg 118): ESA/Hubble & NASA, https://esahubble.org/
- Leonardo the astronaut: Designed by @catalyststuff at https://www.freepik.com/

Finally, a huge thank you to the various space agencies for providing detailed maps of our planets and moons for artists and media works!

About The Author

The author is an aerospace engineer, amateur astronomer, and all-round space enthusiast, with a zest for spreading knowledge through the combination of science and art.

Never stop dreaming!

Milton Keynes UK
Ingram Content Group UK Ltd.
UKRC030659200824
446946UK00004B/1

9781068736414